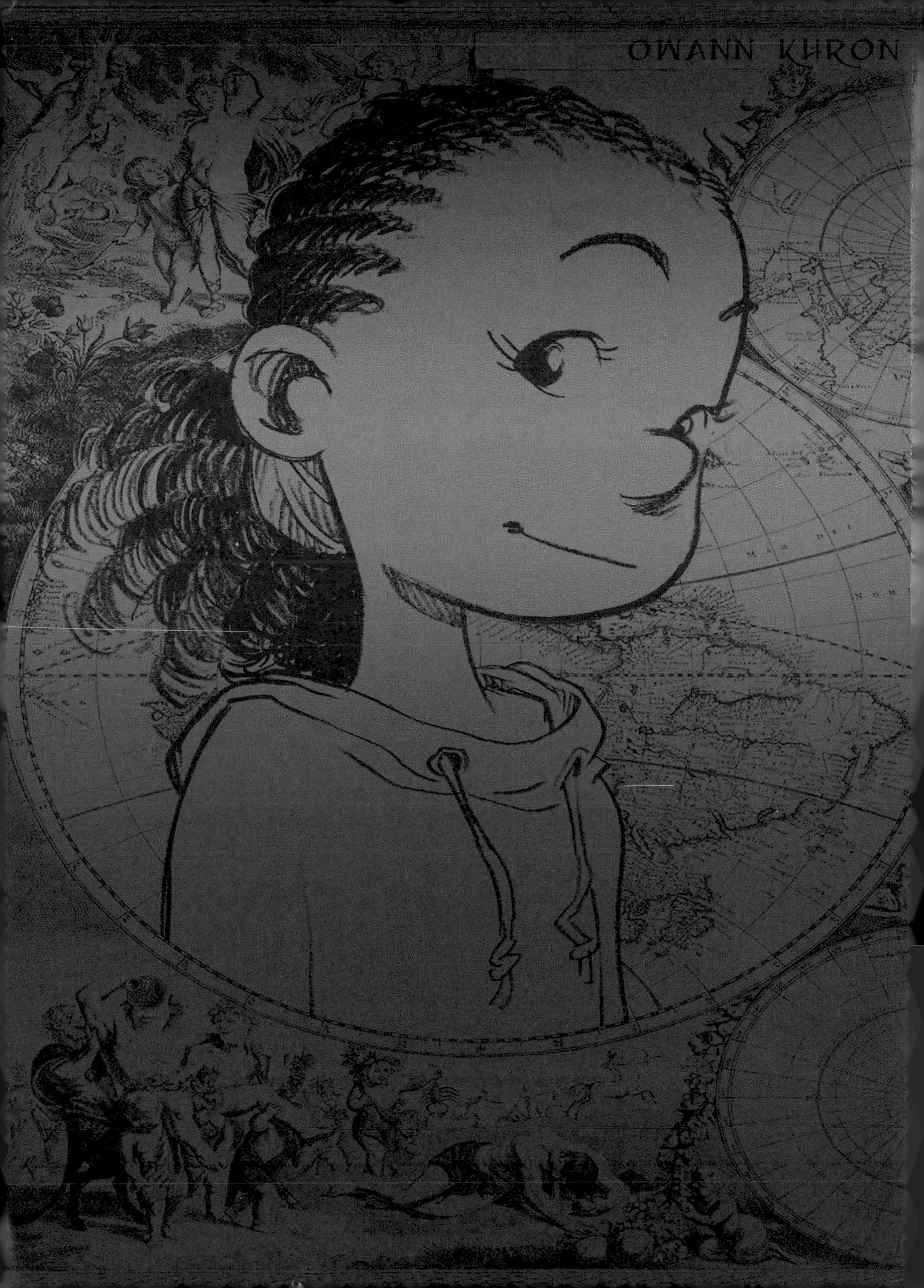
OWANN KURON

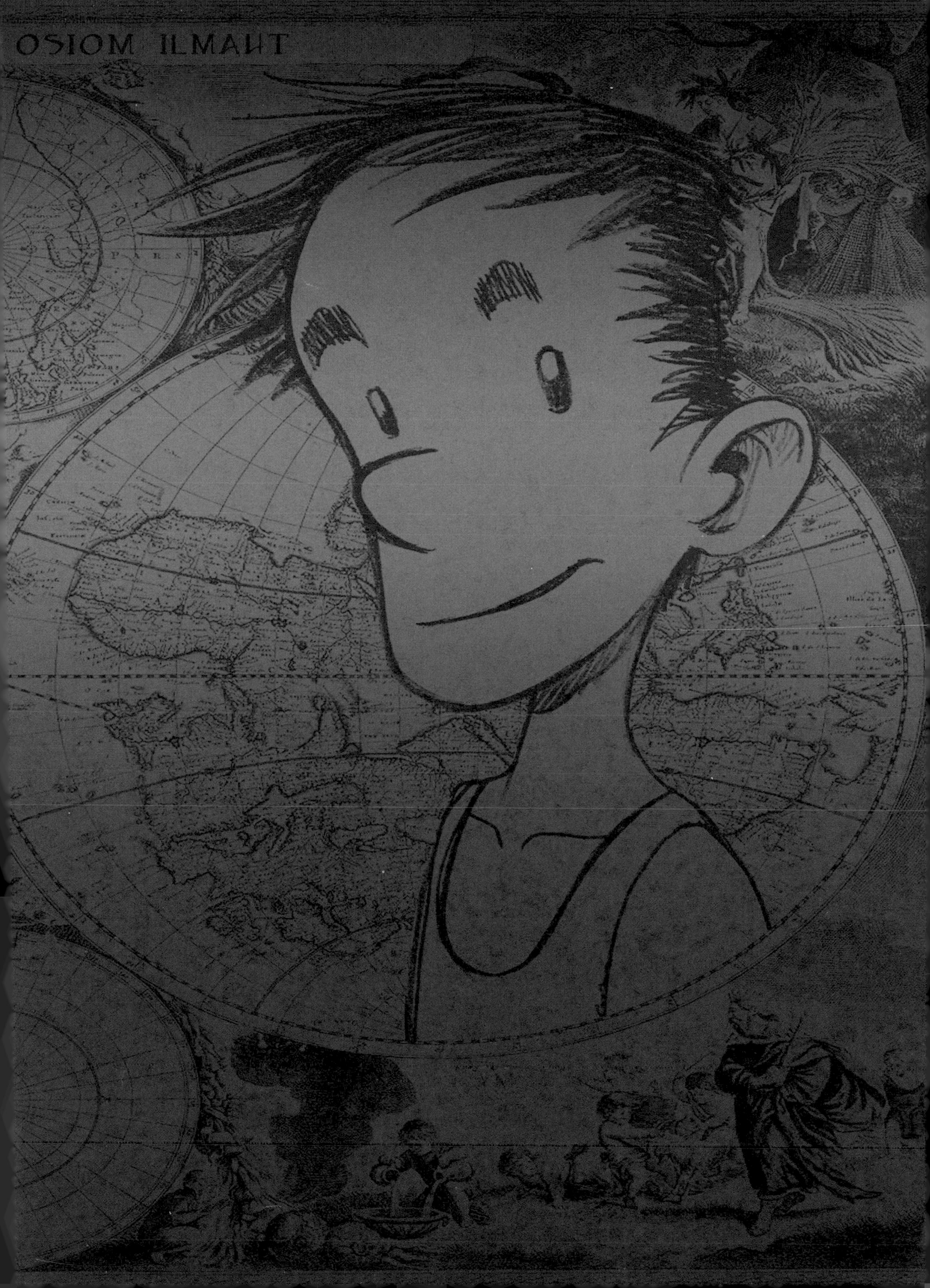

the ElseWhere

CHRONICLES

BOOK TWO
THE SHADOW SPIES

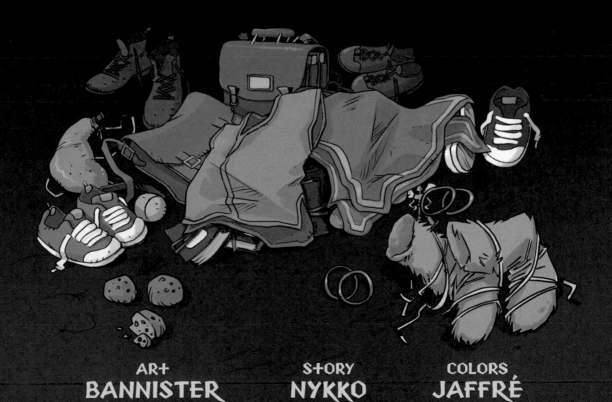

ART
BANNISTER

STORY
NYKKO

COLORS
JAFFRÉ

GRAPHIC UNIVERSE™ • MINNEAPOLIS

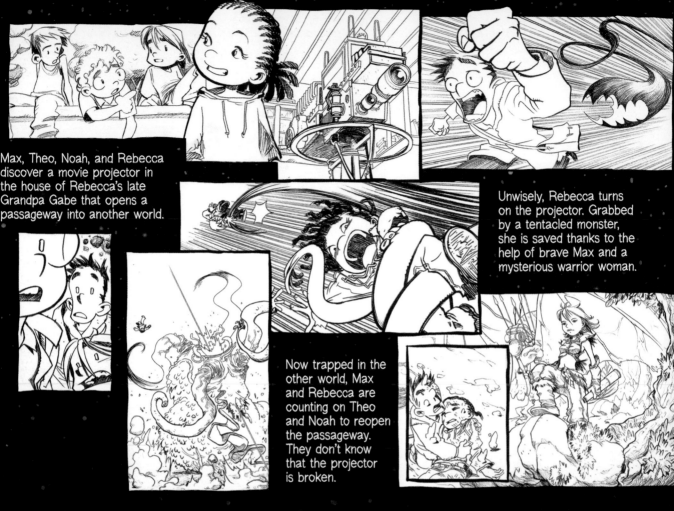

Max, Theo, Noah, and Rebecca discover a movie projector in the house of Rebecca's late Grandpa Gabe that opens a passageway into another world.

Unwisely, Rebecca turns on the projector. Grabbed by a tentacled monster, she is saved thanks to the help of brave Max and a mysterious warrior woman.

Now trapped in the other world, Max and Rebecca are counting on Theo and Noah to reopen the passageway. They don't know that the projector is broken.

THANK you to my PARENTS foR their uNFAiLiNg SuppoRt.

THANk you to DeNiS ANd LauReNce foR theiR sensibLe editoRiAL Advice ANd the 24-houR hotLiNe.

THANk you to my sweet FLORA, without whom this book, At Least the ARt, would be oNLy A Shadow of itseLf.

ANd Next, thANks ALSo to the otheR two guys, because they've doNe A gReAt job too.

—BANNiSteR

To SAbiNe, Léo, ANd Noé

—Nykko

To MAthiLde, ANd thANk you foR youR heLp!

—JAffRé

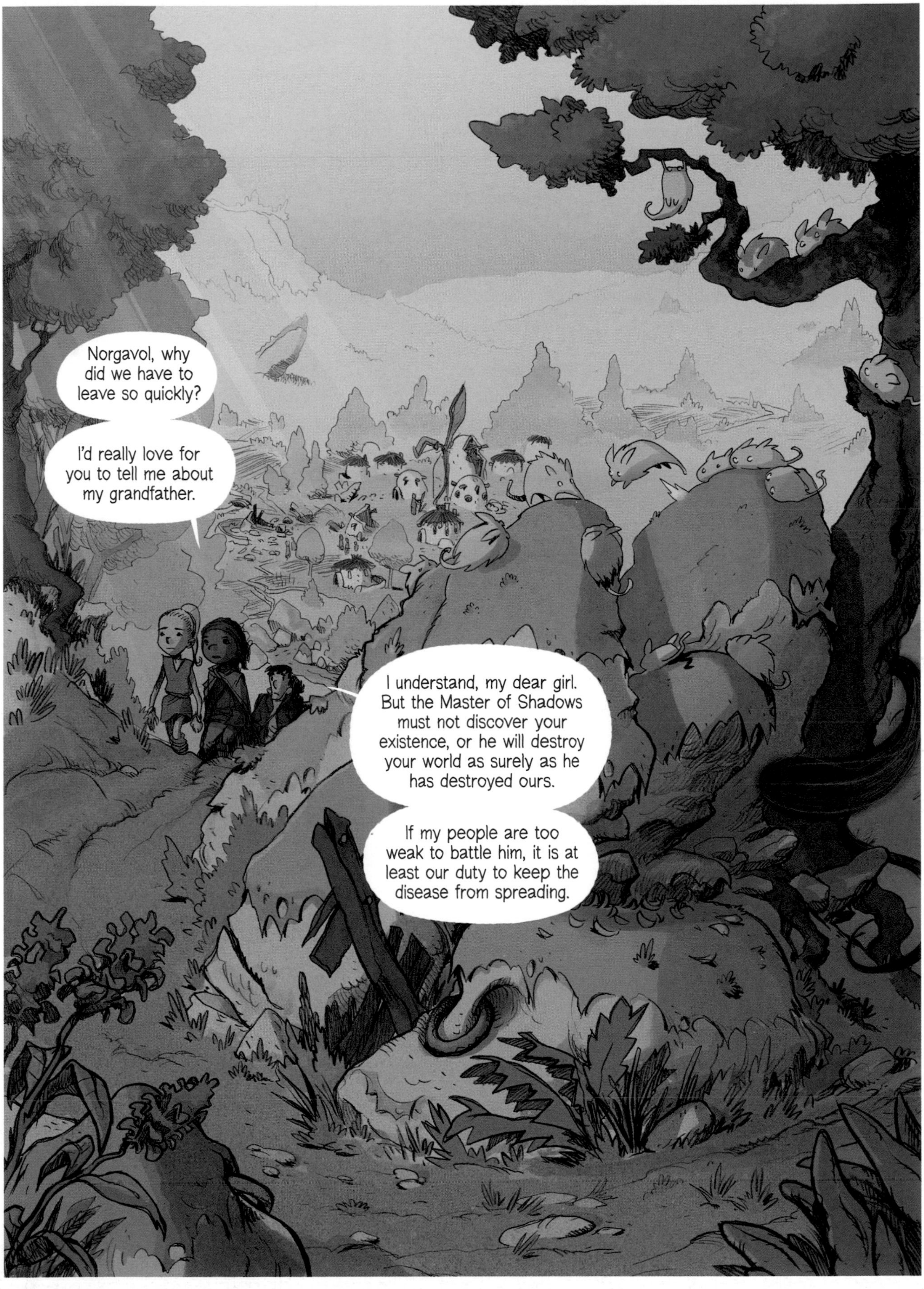
Norgavol, why did we have to leave so quickly?
I'd really love for you to tell me about my grandfather.
I understand, my dear girl. But the Master of Shadows must not discover your existence, or he will destroy your world as surely as he has destroyed ours.
If my people are too weak to battle him, it is at least our duty to keep the disease from spreading.

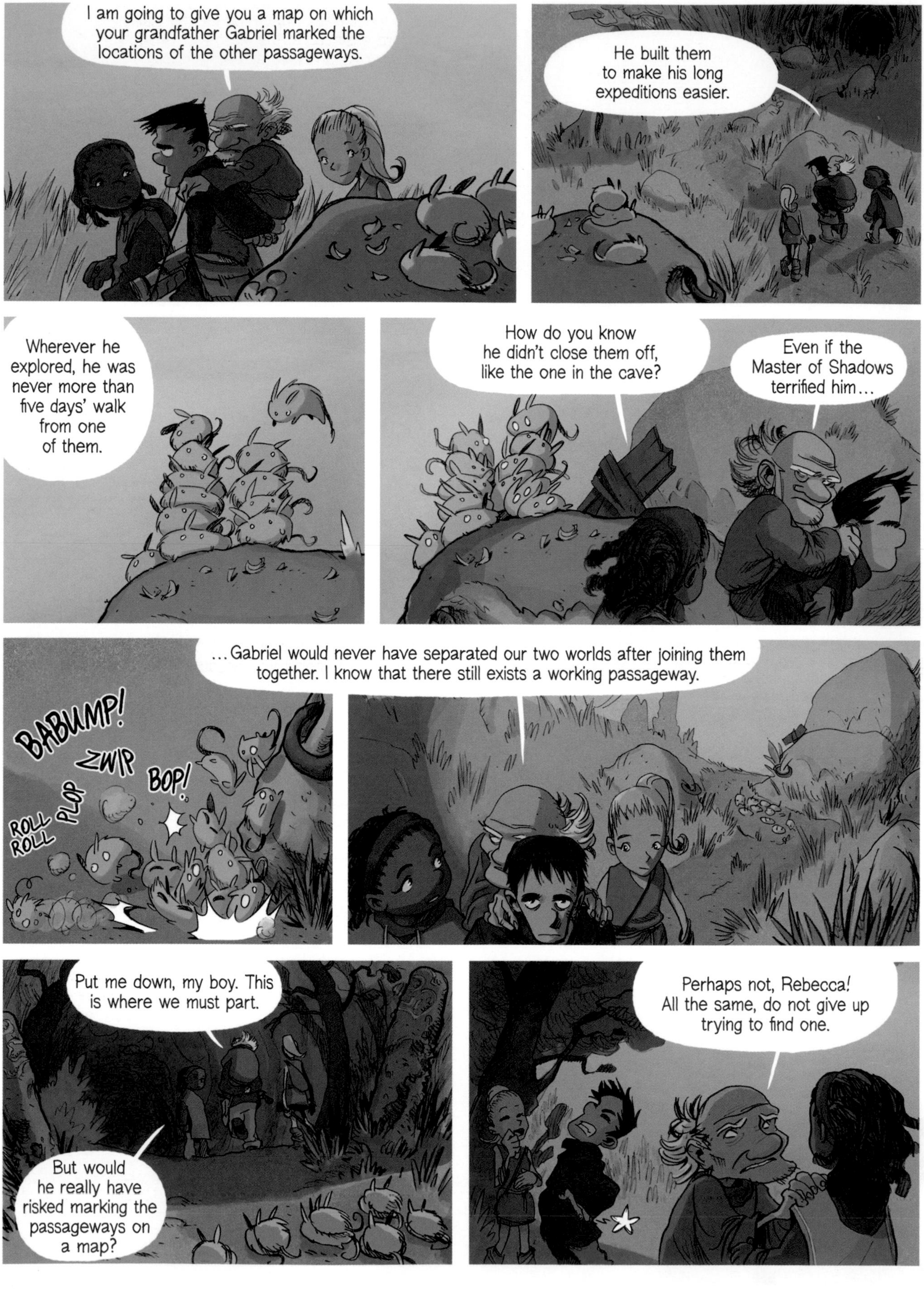
I am going to give you a map on which your grandfather Gabriel marked the locations of the other passageways.
He built them to make his long expeditions easier.
Wherever he explored, he was never more than five days' walk from one of them.
How do you know he didn't close them off, like the one in the cave?
Even if the Master of Shadows terrified him...
...Gabriel would never have separated our two worlds after joining them together. I know that there still exists a working passageway.
BABUMP!
ZWIP
BOP!
PLOP
ROLL ROLL
Put me down, my boy. This is where we must part.
But would he really have risked marking the passageways on a map?
Perhaps not, Rebecca! All the same, do not give up trying to find one.

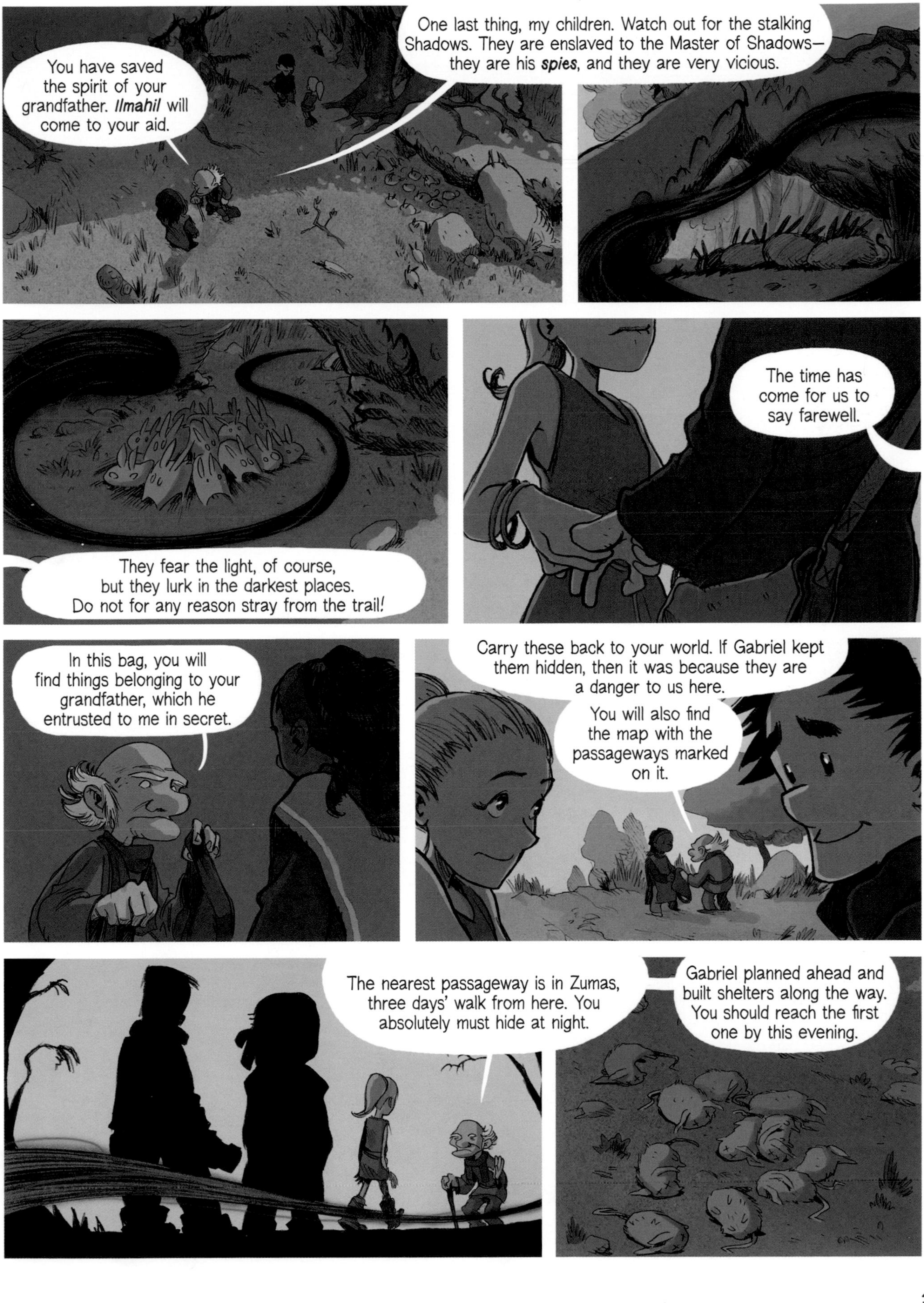
You have saved the spirit of your grandfather. *Ilmahil* will come to your aid.
One last thing, my children. Watch out for the stalking Shadows. They are enslaved to the Master of Shadows—they are his *spies*, and they are very vicious.
They fear the light, of course, but they lurk in the darkest places. Do not for any reason stray from the trail!
The time has come for us to say farewell.
In this bag, you will find things belonging to your grandfather, which he entrusted to me in secret.
Carry these back to your world. If Gabriel kept them hidden, then it was because they are a danger to us here.
You will also find the map with the passageways marked on it.
The nearest passageway is in Zumas, three days' walk from here. You absolutely must hide at night.
Gabriel planned ahead and built shelters along the way. You should reach the first one by this evening.

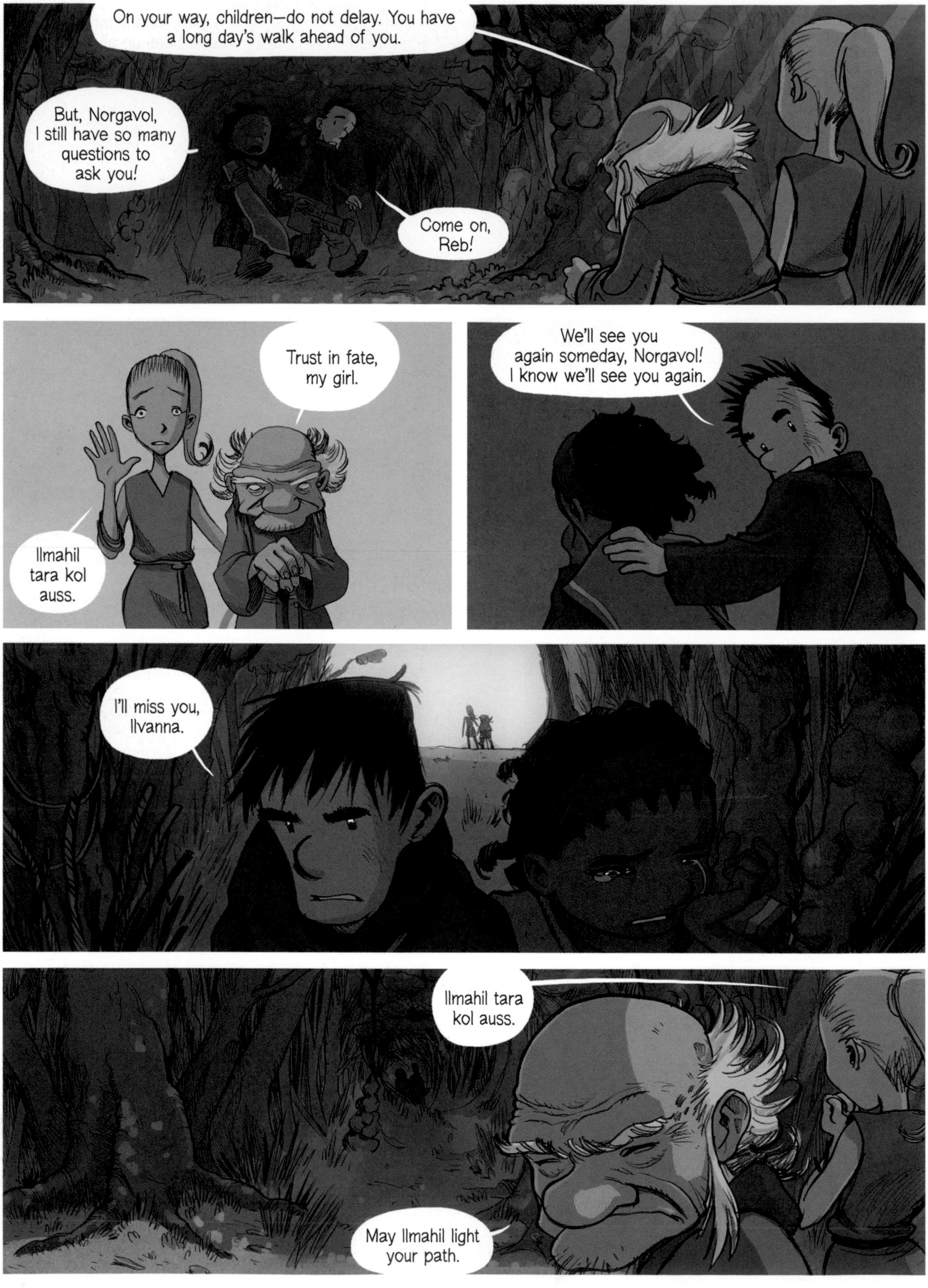
On your way, children—do not delay. You have a long day's walk ahead of you.
But, Norgavol, I still have so many questions to ask you!
Come on, Reb!
Trust in fate, my girl.
Ilmahil tara kol auss.
We'll see you again someday, Norgavol! I know we'll see you again.
I'll miss you, Ilvanna.
Ilmahil tara kol auss.
May Ilmahil light your path.

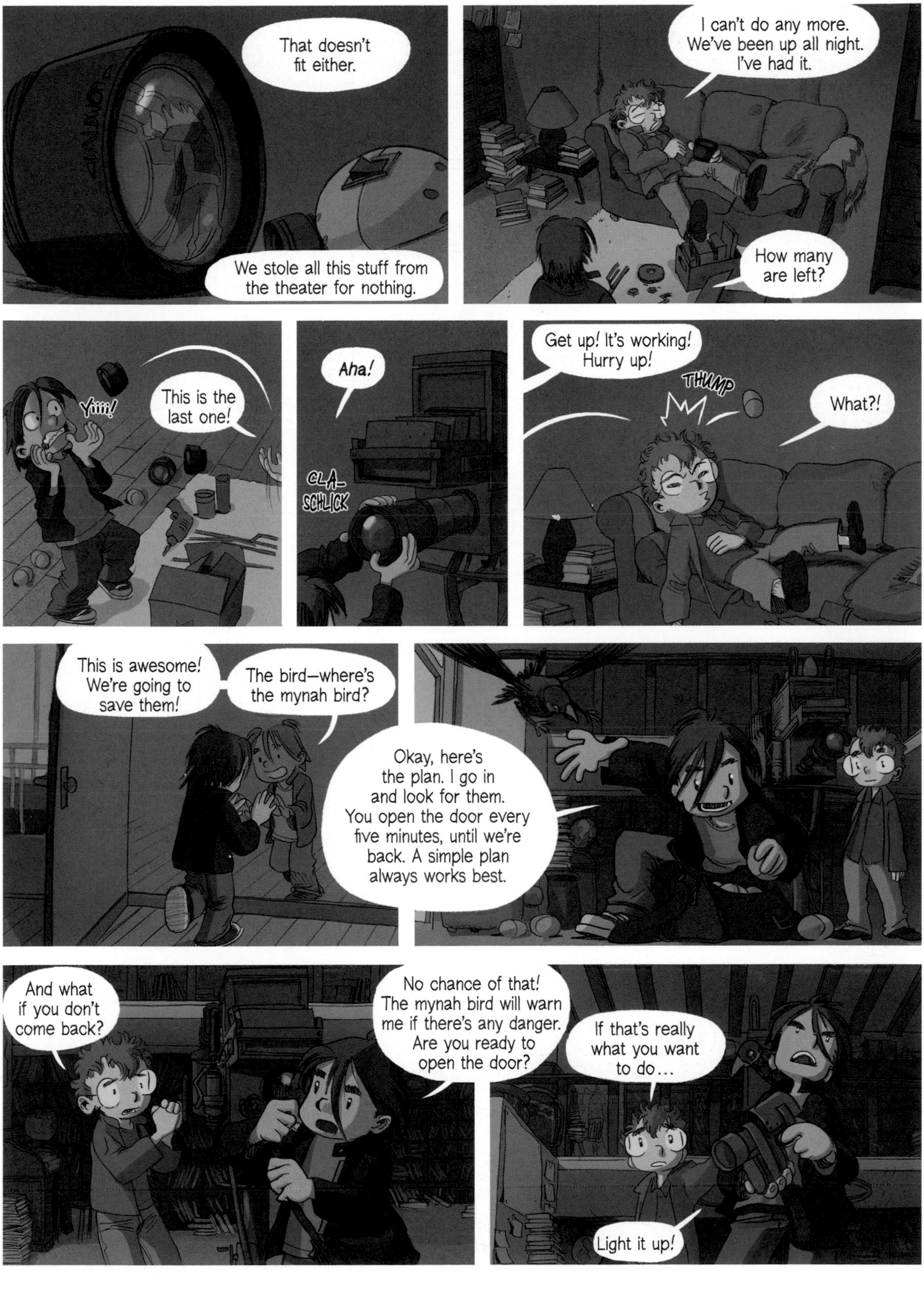
That doesn't fit either.
We stole all this stuff from the theater for nothing.
I can't do any more. We've been up all night. I've had it.
How many are left?
Yiiii!
This is the last one!
Aha!
CLA-SCHLICK
Get up! It's working! Hurry up!
THUMP
What?!
This is awesome! We're going to save them!
The bird—where's the mynah bird?
Okay, here's the plan. I go in and look for them. You open the door every five minutes, until we're back. A simple plan always works best.
And what if you don't come back?
No chance of that! The mynah bird will warn me if there's any danger. Are you ready to open the door?
If that's really what you want to do…
Light it up!

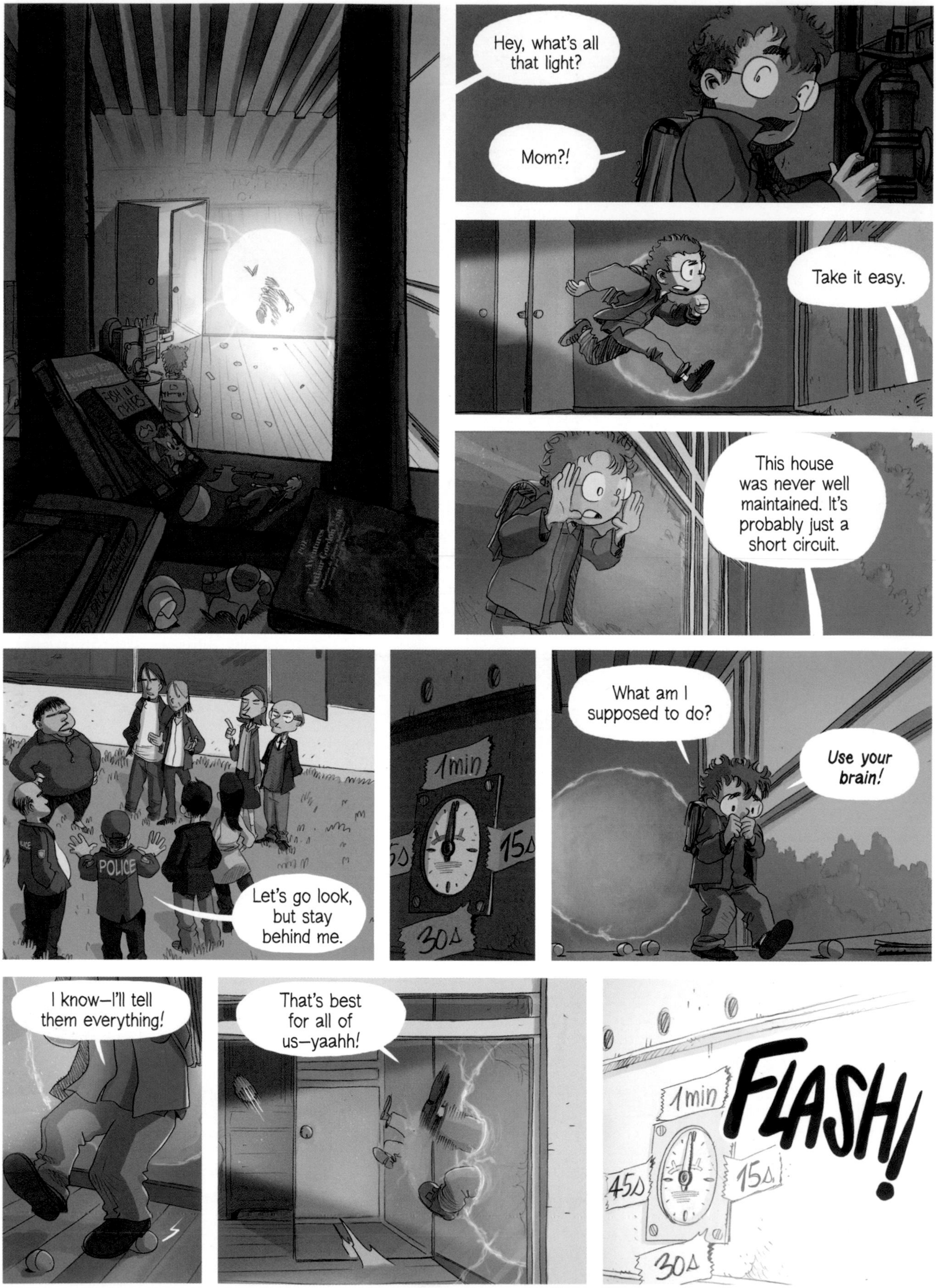

Hey, what's all that light?
Mom?!
Take it easy.
This house was never well maintained. It's probably just a short circuit.
POLICE
Let's go look, but stay behind me.
1min
What am I supposed to do?
Use your brain!
I know—I'll tell them everything!
That's best for all of us—yaahh!
1min
FLASH!

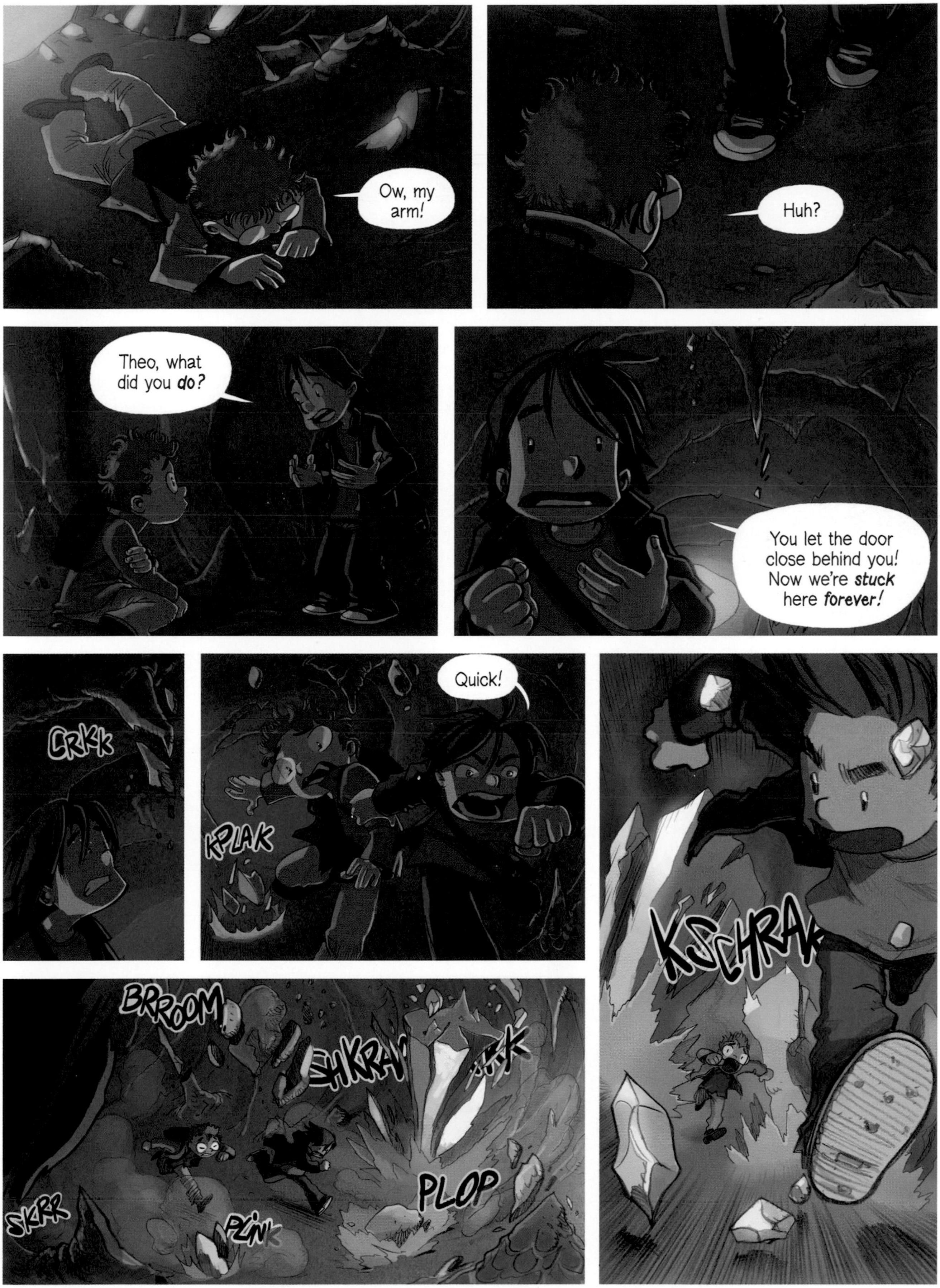
Ow, my arm!
Huh?
Theo, what did you *do?*
You let the door close behind you! Now we're *stuck* here *forever!*
CRKK
Quick!
KPLAK
KSCHRAK
BRROOM
PLOP
SKRR
PLINK

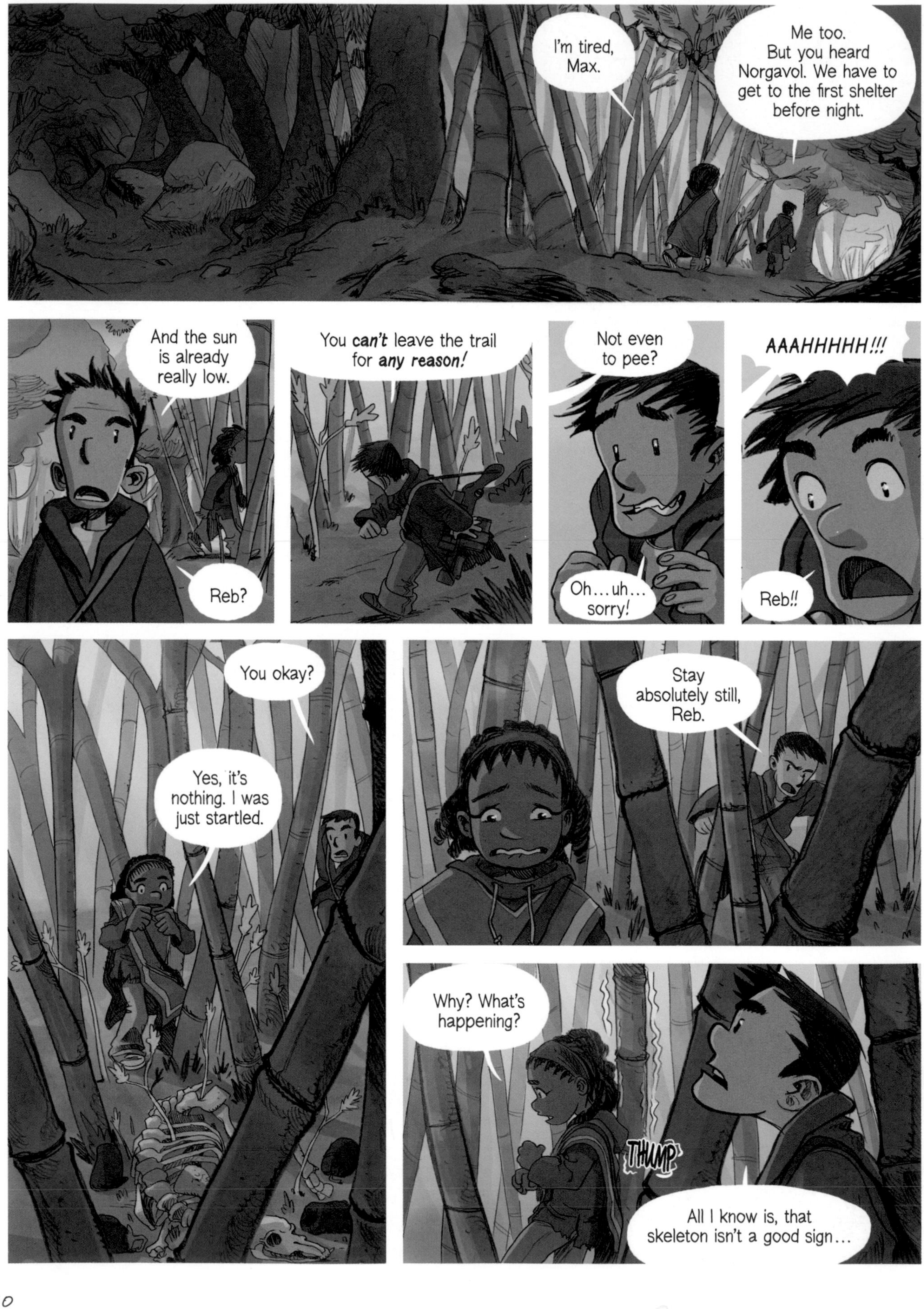
I'm tired, Max.
Me too. But you heard Norgavol. We have to get to the first shelter before night.
And the sun is already really low.
Reb?
You **can't** leave the trail for **any reason!**
Not even to pee?
Oh... uh... sorry!
AAAHHHHH!!!
Reb!!
You okay?
Yes, it's nothing. I was just startled.
Stay absolutely still, Reb.
Why? What's happening?
THUMP
All I know is, that skeleton isn't a good sign...

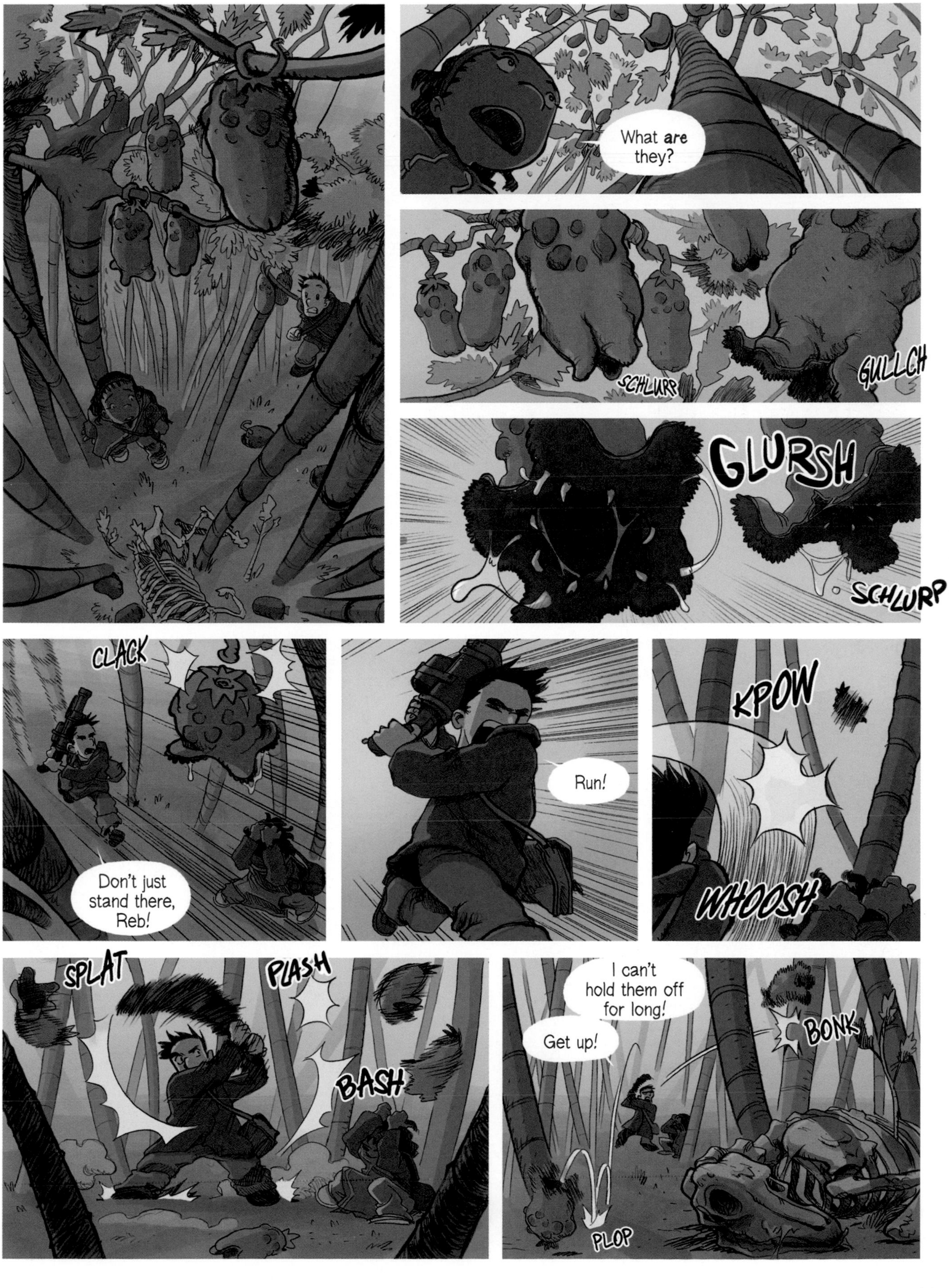
What are they?
SCHLURP
GULLCH
GLURSH
SCHLURP
CLACK
Don't just stand there, Reb!
Run!
KPOW
WHOOSH
SPLAT
PLASH
BASH
I can't hold them off for long!
Get up!
BONK
PLOP

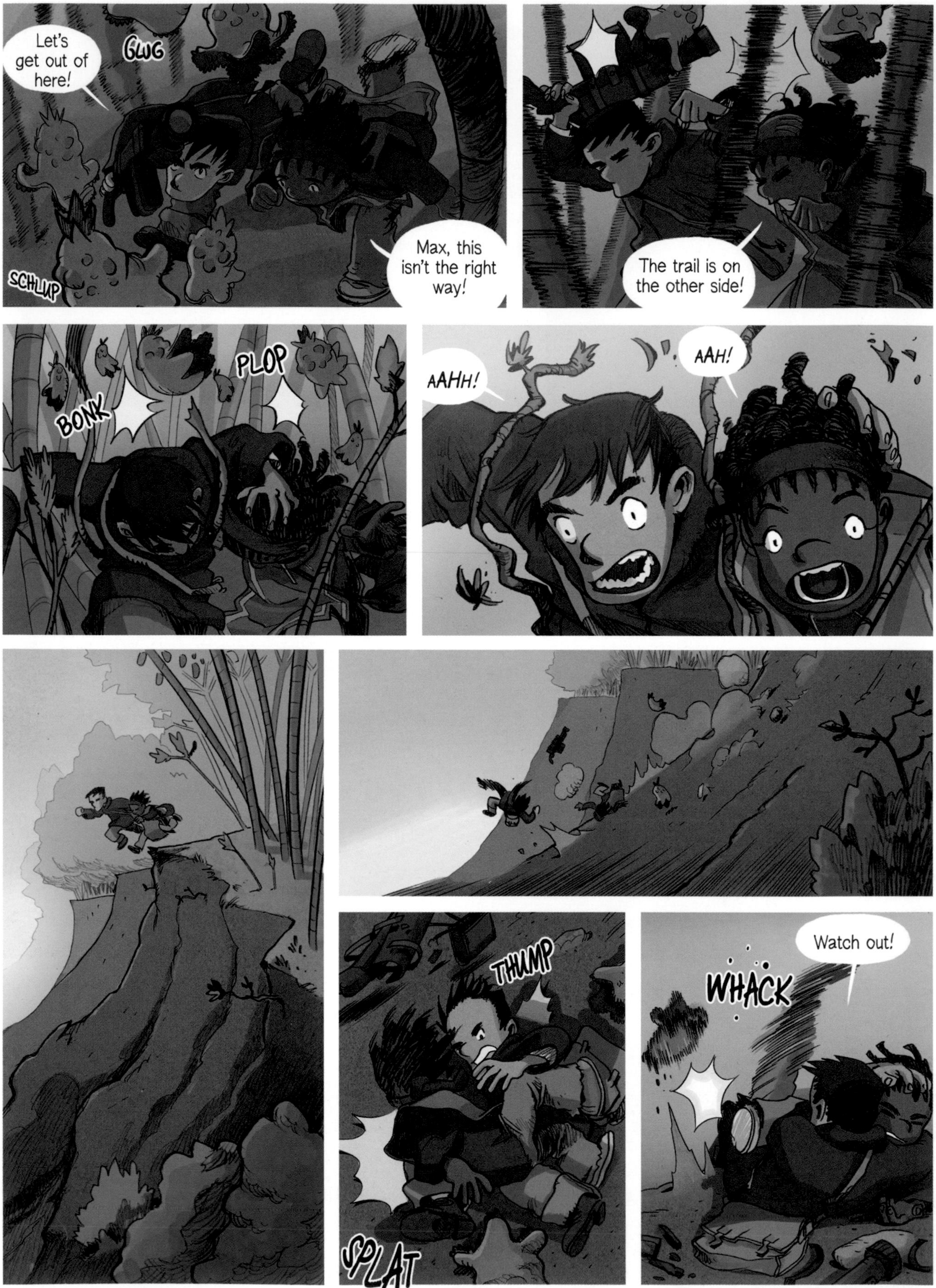
Let's get out of here!
GLUG
SCHLUP
Max, this isn't the right way!
The trail is on the other side!
BONK
PLOP
AAHH!
AAH!
THUMP
SPLAT
WHACK
Watch out!

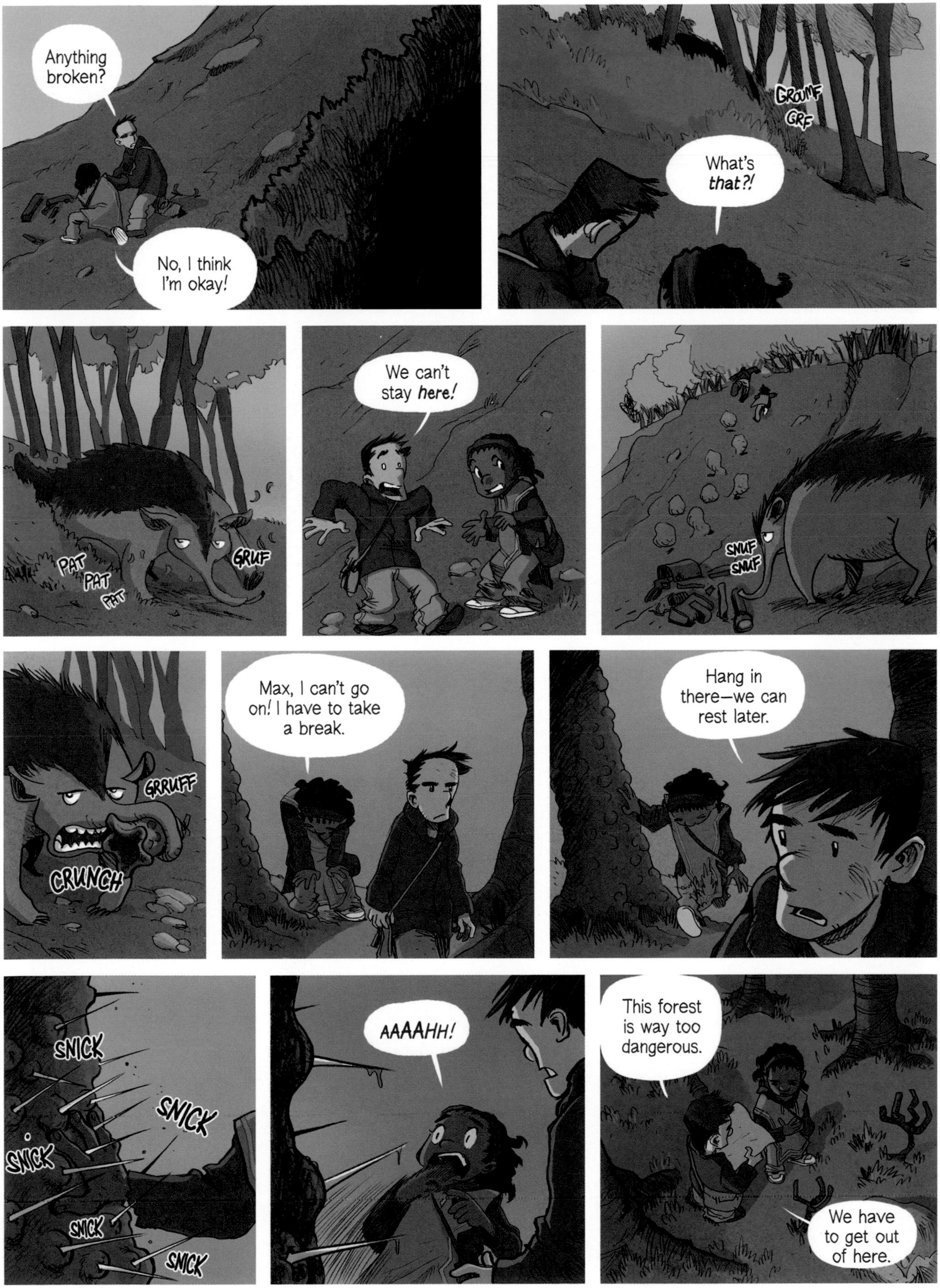
Anything broken?
No, I think I'm okay!
GROUMF
GRF
What's *that?!*
PAT
PAT
PAT
GRUF
We can't stay *here!*
SNUF
SNUF
GRRUFF
CRUNCH
Max, I can't go on! I have to take a break.
Hang in there—we can rest later.
SNICK
SNICK
SNICK
SNICK
SNICK
AAAAHH!
This forest is way too dangerous.
We have to get out of here.

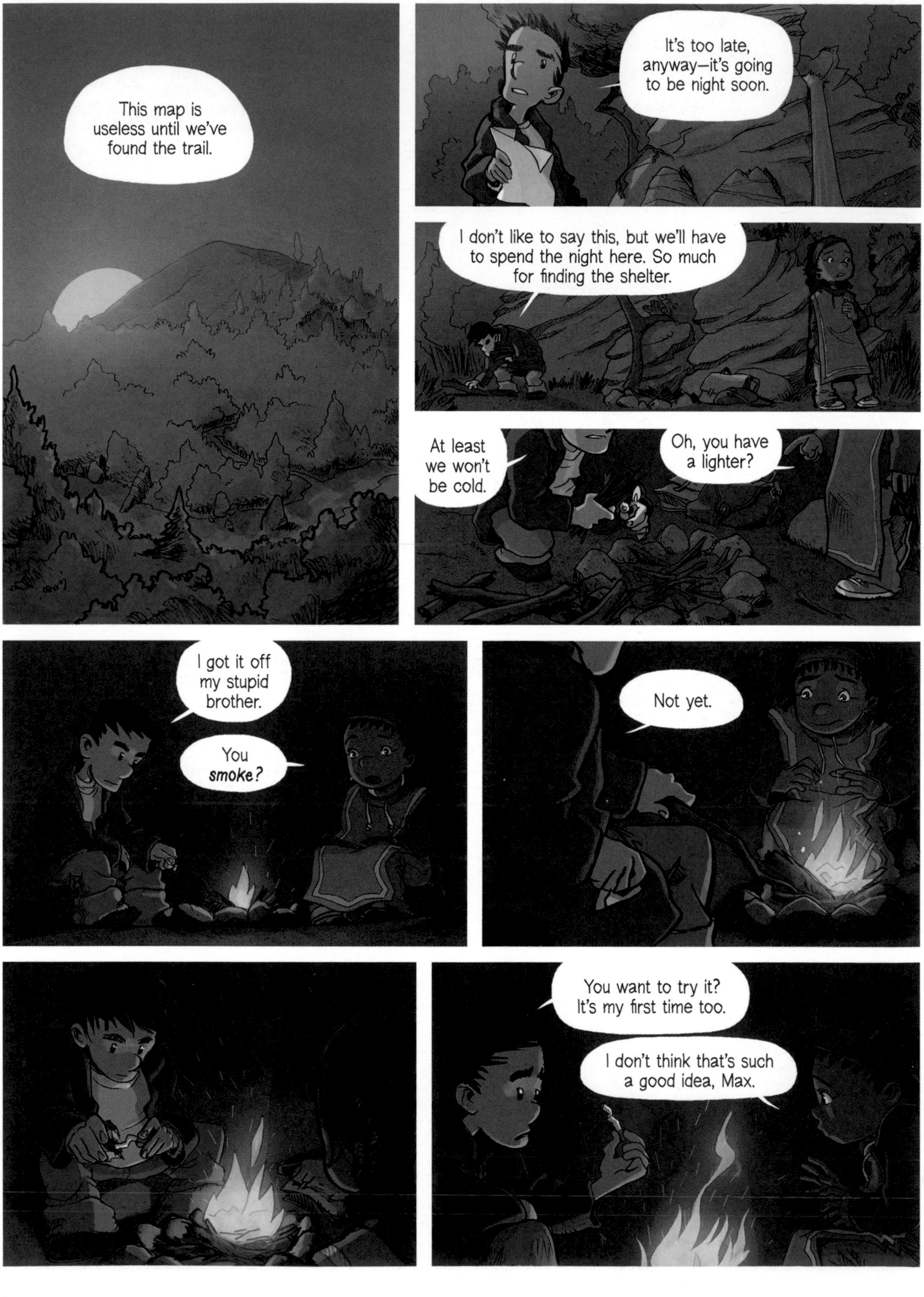
This map is useless until we've found the trail.
It's too late, anyway—it's going to be night soon.
I don't like to say this, but we'll have to spend the night here. So much for finding the shelter.
At least we won't be cold.
Oh, you have a lighter?
I got it off my stupid brother.
You *smoke?*
Not yet.
You want to try it? It's my first time too.
I don't think that's such a good idea, Max.

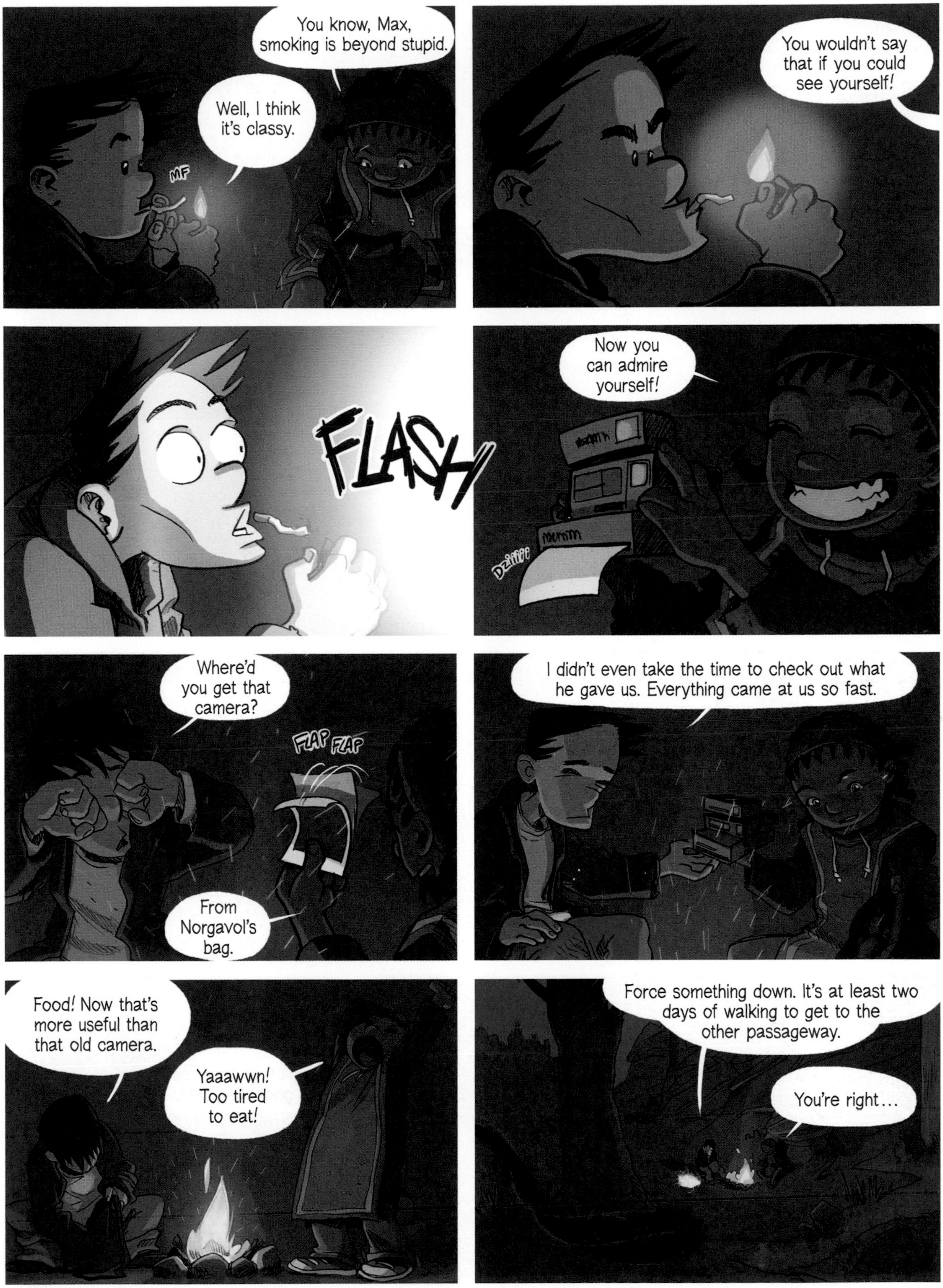
You know, Max, smoking is beyond stupid.
Well, I think it's classy.
MF
You wouldn't say that if you could see yourself!
FLASH
Now you can admire yourself!
Dziiiii
Where'd you get that camera?
FLAP FLAP
From Norgavol's bag.
I didn't even take the time to check out what he gave us. Everything came at us so fast.
Food! Now that's more useful than that old camera.
Yaaawwn! Too tired to eat!
Force something down. It's at least two days of walking to get to the other passageway.
You're right...

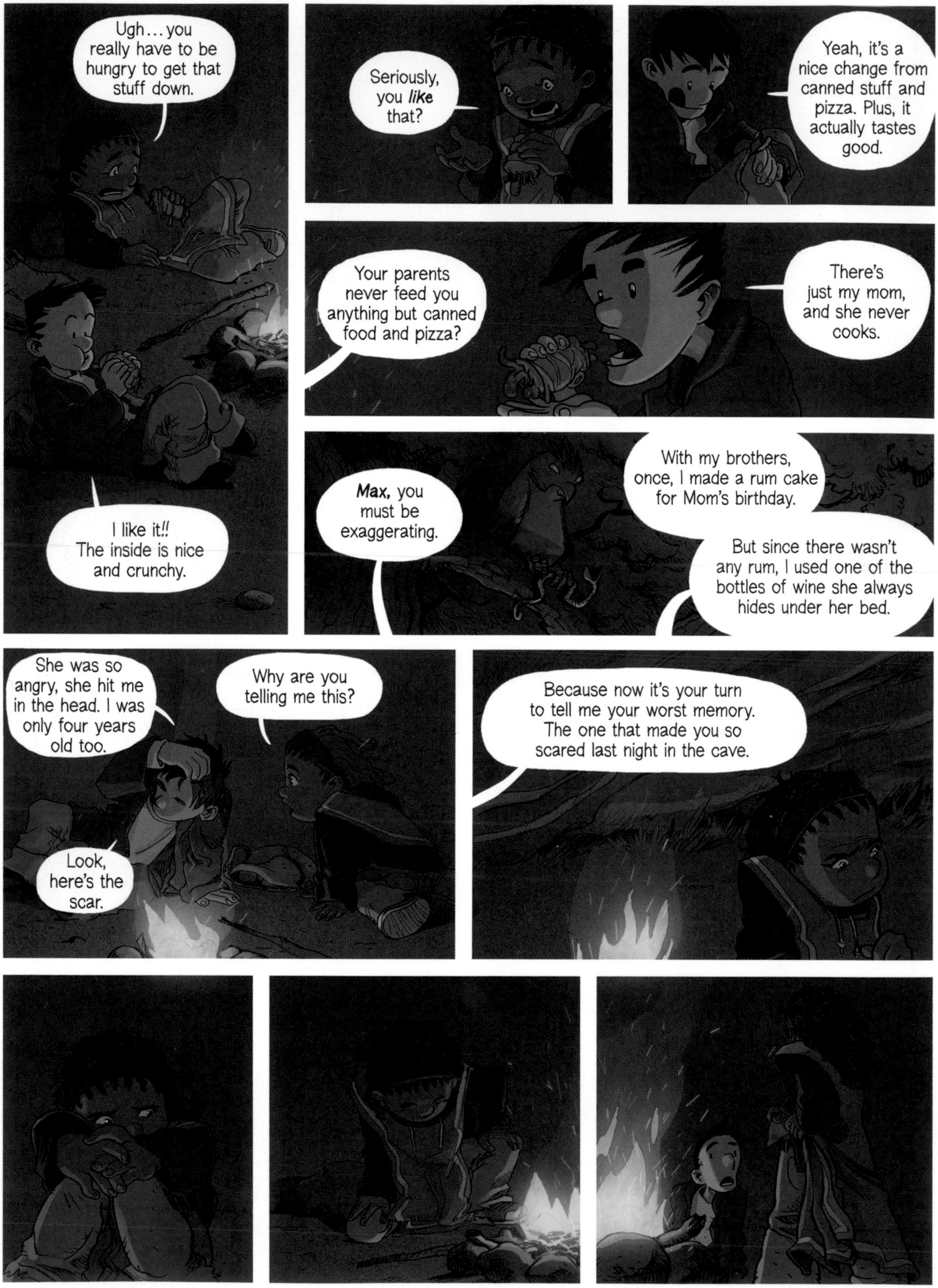

Ugh... you really have to be hungry to get that stuff down.
I like it!! The inside is nice and crunchy.
Seriously, you *like* that?
Yeah, it's a nice change from canned stuff and pizza. Plus, it actually tastes good.
Your parents never feed you anything but canned food and pizza?
There's just my mom, and she never cooks.
Max, you must be exaggerating.
With my brothers, once, I made a rum cake for Mom's birthday.
But since there wasn't any rum, I used one of the bottles of wine she always hides under her bed.
She was so angry, she hit me in the head. I was only four years old too.
Look, here's the scar.
Why are you telling me this?
Because now it's your turn to tell me your worst memory. The one that made you so scared last night in the cave.

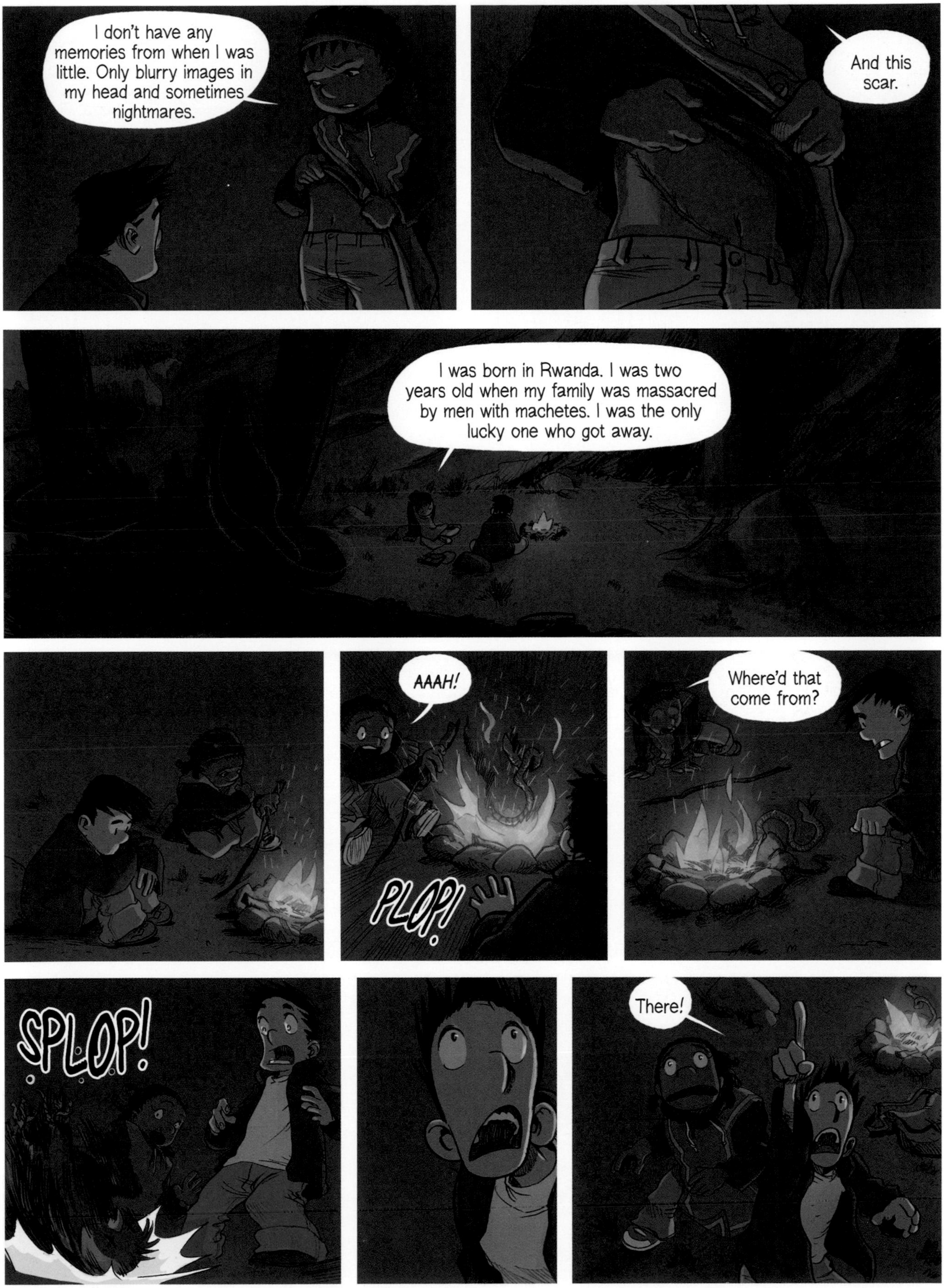
I don't have any memories from when I was little. Only blurry images in my head and sometimes nightmares.
And this scar.
I was born in Rwanda. I was two years old when my family was massacred by men with machetes. I was the only lucky one who got away.
AAAH!
PLOP!
Where'd that come from?
SPLOP!
There!

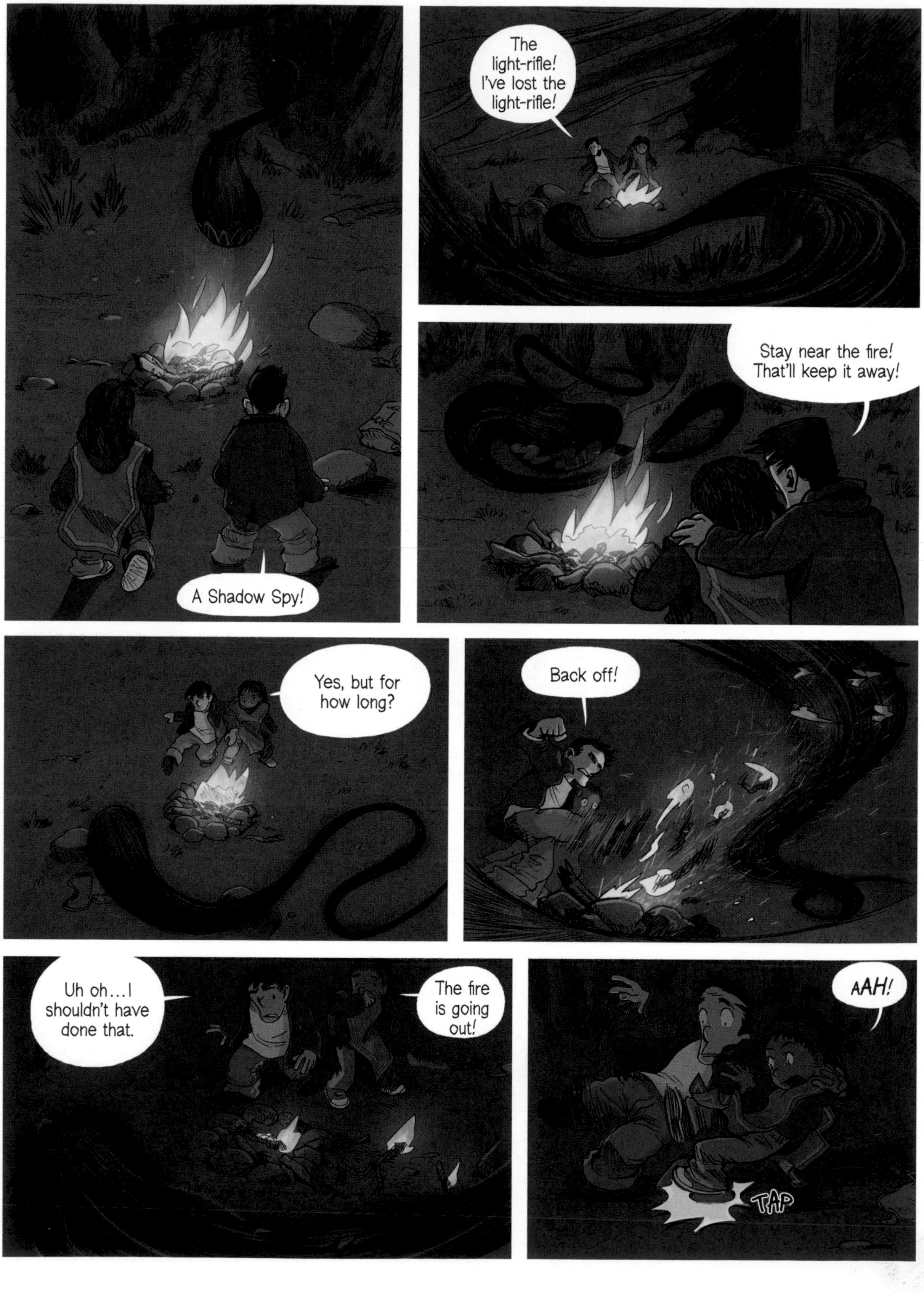
A Shadow Spy!
The light-rifle! I've lost the light-rifle!
Stay near the fire! That'll keep it away!
Yes, but for how long?
Back off!
Uh oh... I shouldn't have done that.
The fire is going out!
AAH!
TAP

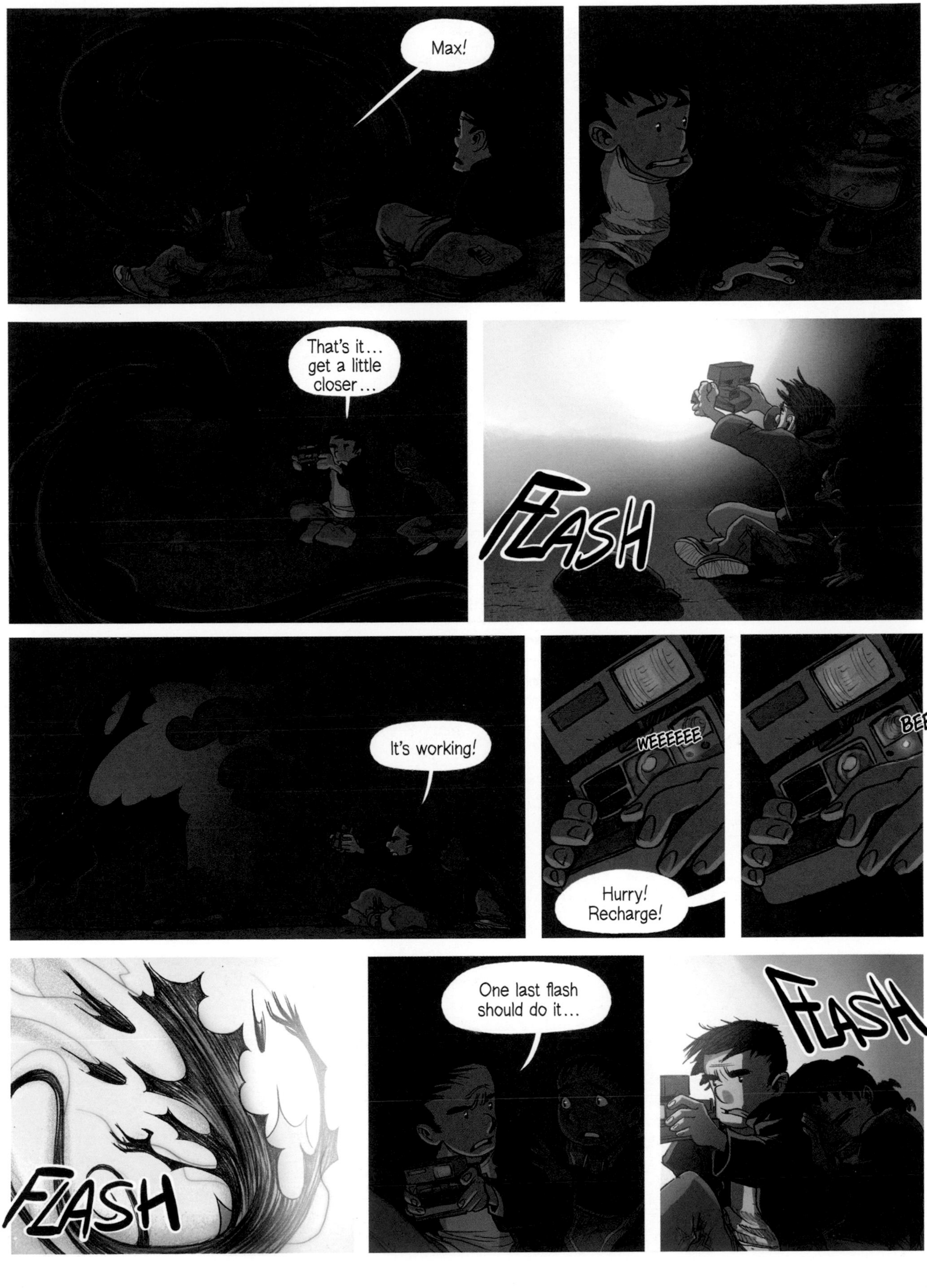
Max!
That's it... get a little closer...
FLASH
It's working!
WEEEEEE
Hurry! Recharge!
BEEP
FLASH
One last flash should do it...
FLASH

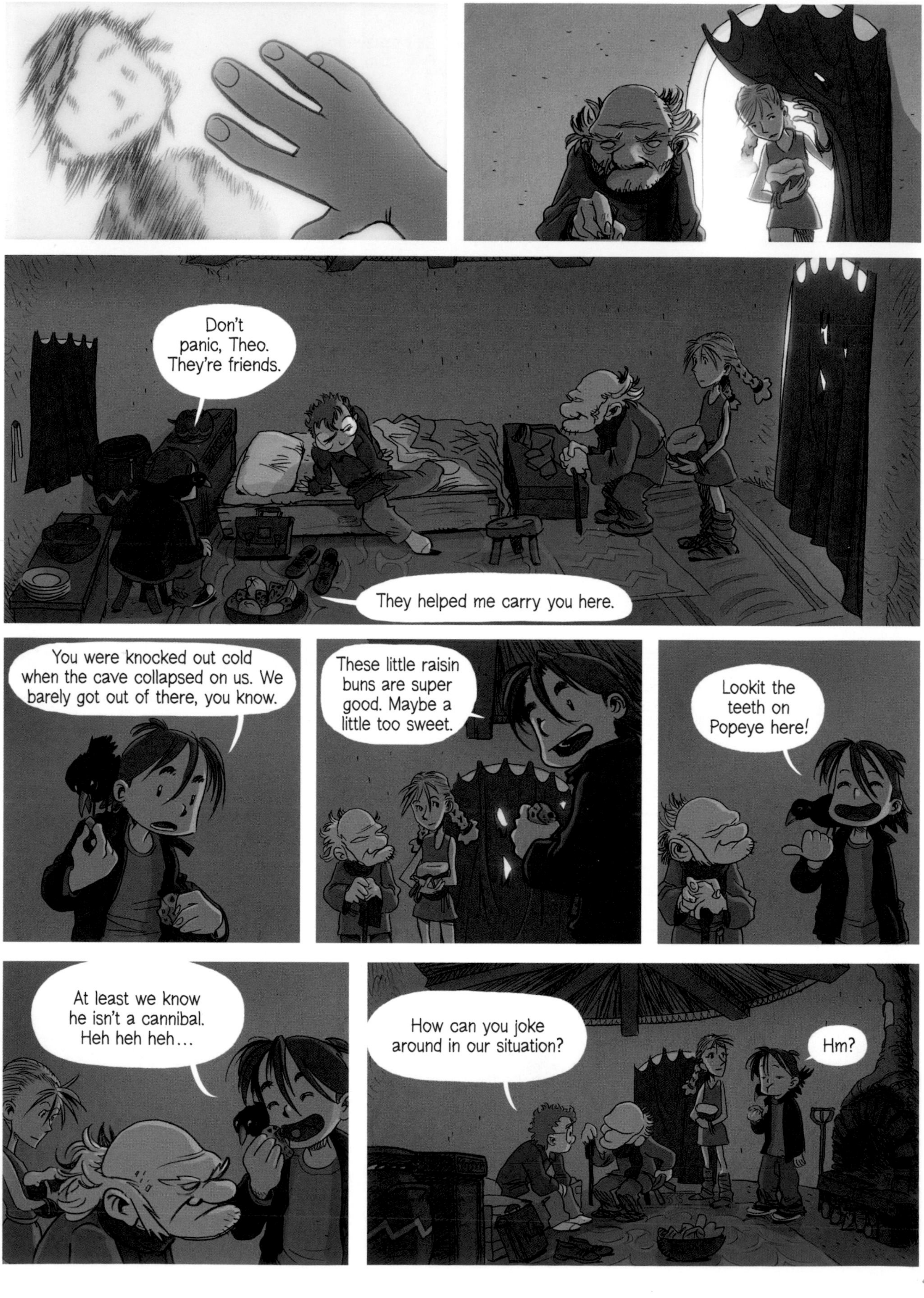
Don't panic, Theo. They're friends.
They helped me carry you here.
You were knocked out cold when the cave collapsed on us. We barely got out of there, you know.
These little raisin buns are super good. Maybe a little too sweet.
Lookit the teeth on Popeye here!
At least we know he isn't a cannibal. Heh heh heh...
How can you joke around in our situation?
Hm?

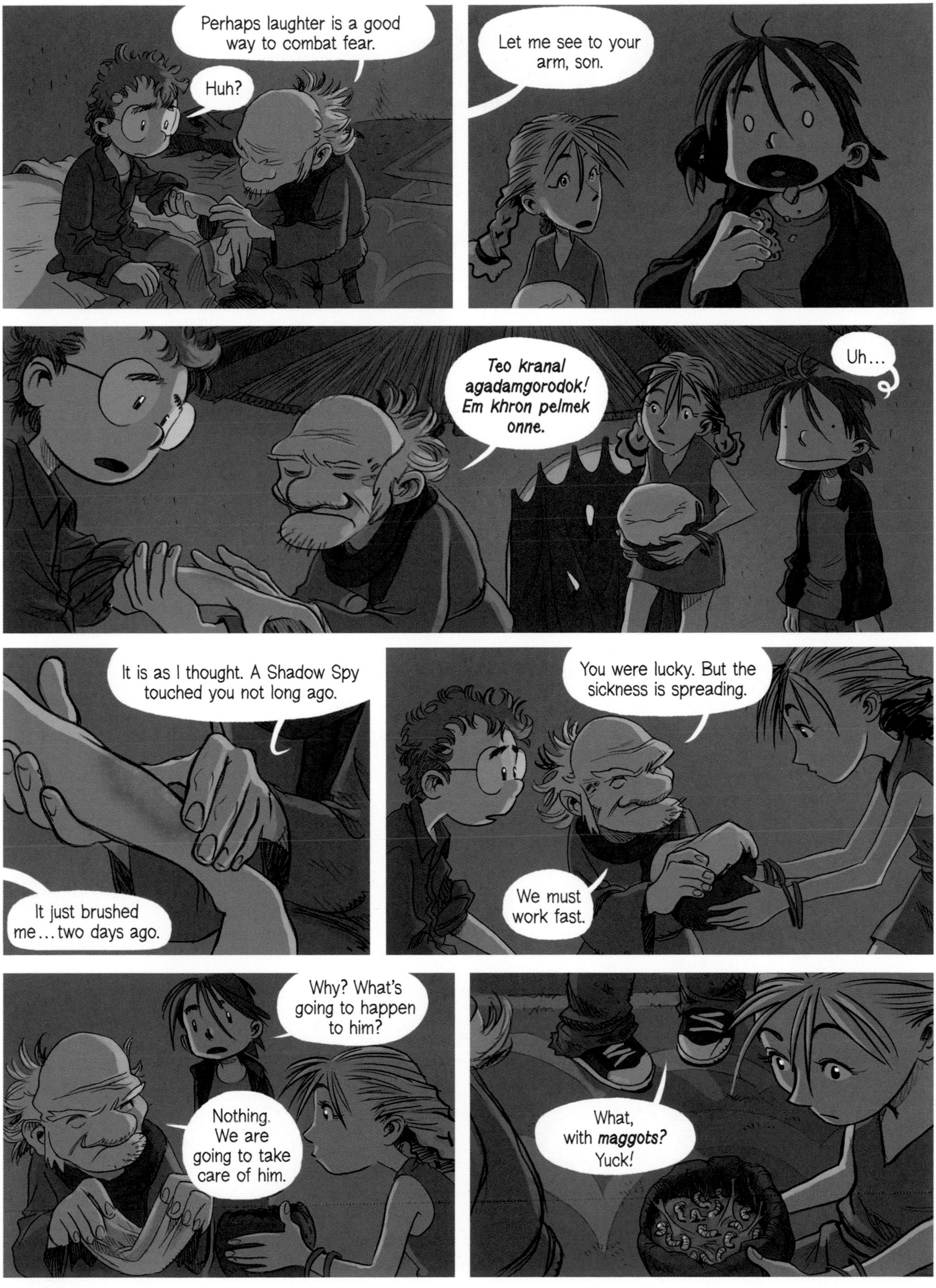
Perhaps laughter is a good way to combat fear.
Huh?
Let me see to your arm, son.
Teo kranal agadamgorodok! Em khron pelmek onne.
Uh...
It is as I thought. A Shadow Spy touched you not long ago.
It just brushed me... two days ago.
You were lucky. But the sickness is spreading.
We must work fast.
Why? What's going to happen to him?
Nothing. We are going to take care of him.
What, with maggots? Yuck!

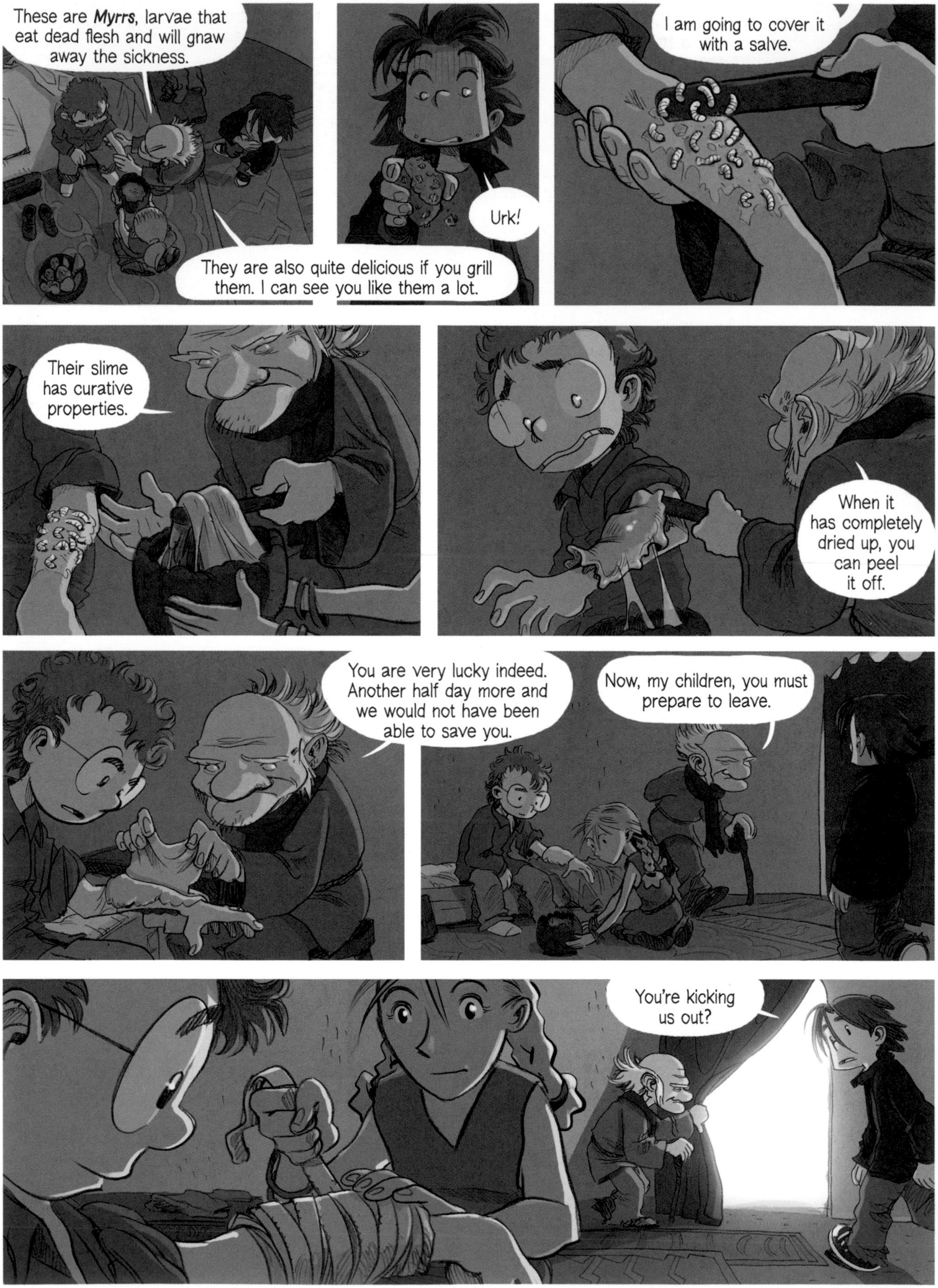
These are **Myrrs**, larvae that eat dead flesh and will gnaw away the sickness.
Urk!
They are also quite delicious if you grill them. I can see you like them a lot.
I am going to cover it with a salve.
Their slime has curative properties.
When it has completely dried up, you can peel it off.
You are very lucky indeed. Another half day more and we would not have been able to save you.
Now, my children, you must prepare to leave.
You're kicking us out?

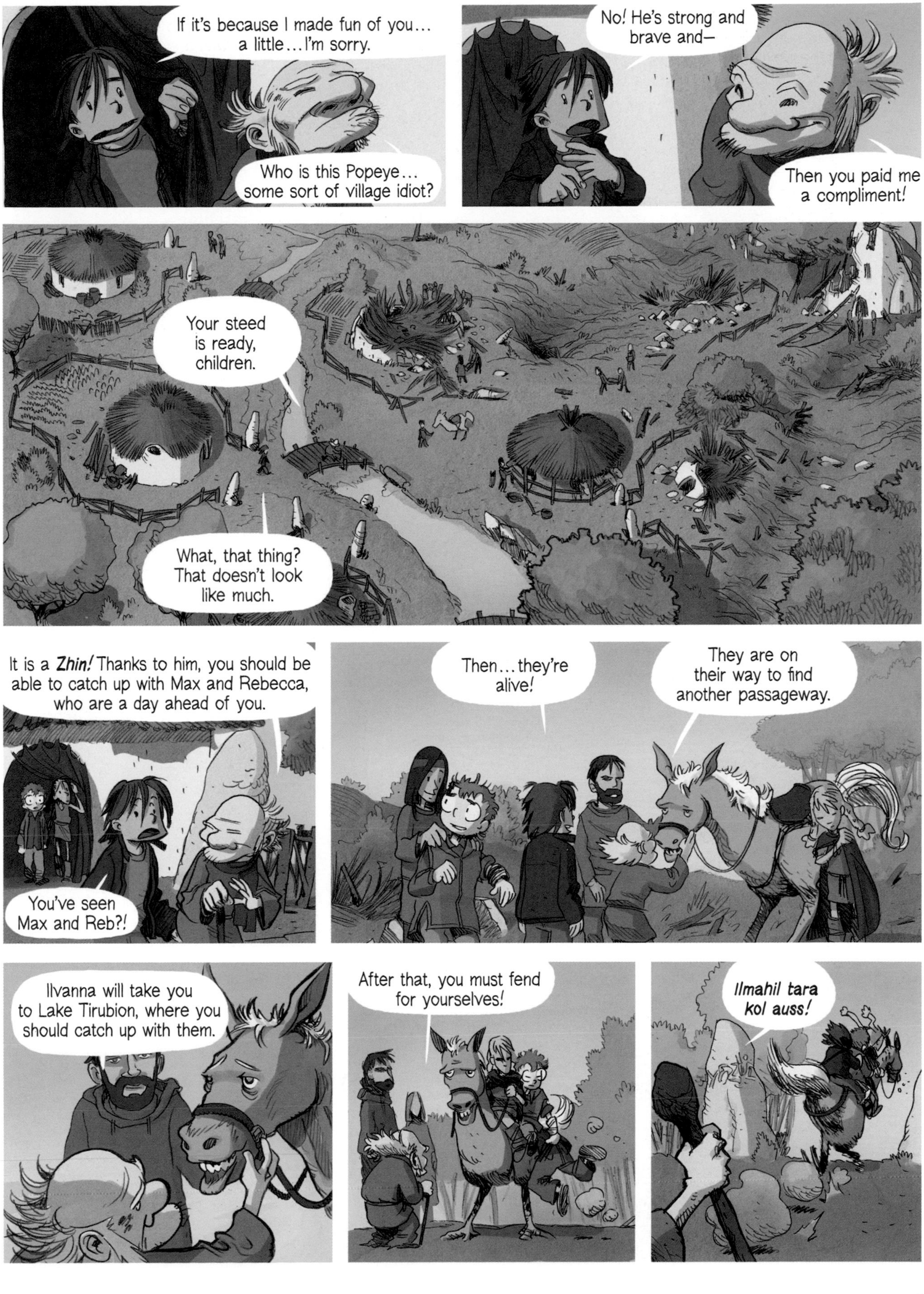
If it's because I made fun of you... a little...I'm sorry.
Who is this Popeye... some sort of village idiot?
No! He's strong and brave and—
Then you paid me a compliment!
Your steed is ready, children.
What, that thing? That doesn't look like much.
It is a *Zhin!* Thanks to him, you should be able to catch up with Max and Rebecca, who are a day ahead of you.
You've seen Max and Reb?!
Then...they're alive!
They are on their way to find another passageway.
Ilvanna will take you to Lake Tirubion, where you should catch up with them.
After that, you must fend for yourselves!
Ilmahil tara kol auss!

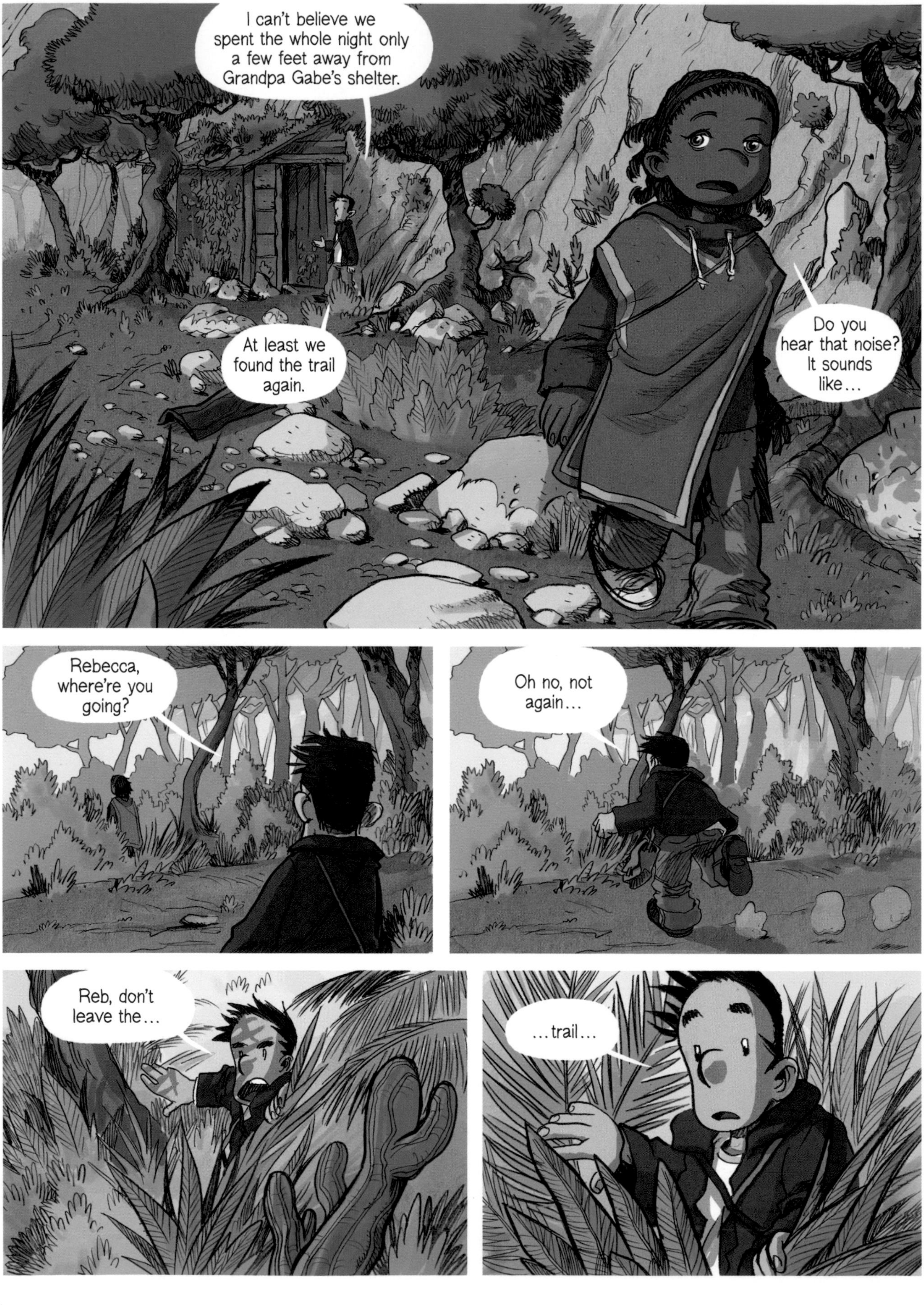
I can't believe we spent the whole night only a few feet away from Grandpa Gabe's shelter.
At least we found the trail again.
Do you hear that noise? It sounds like...
Rebecca, where're you going?
Oh no, not again...
Reb, don't leave the...
...trail...

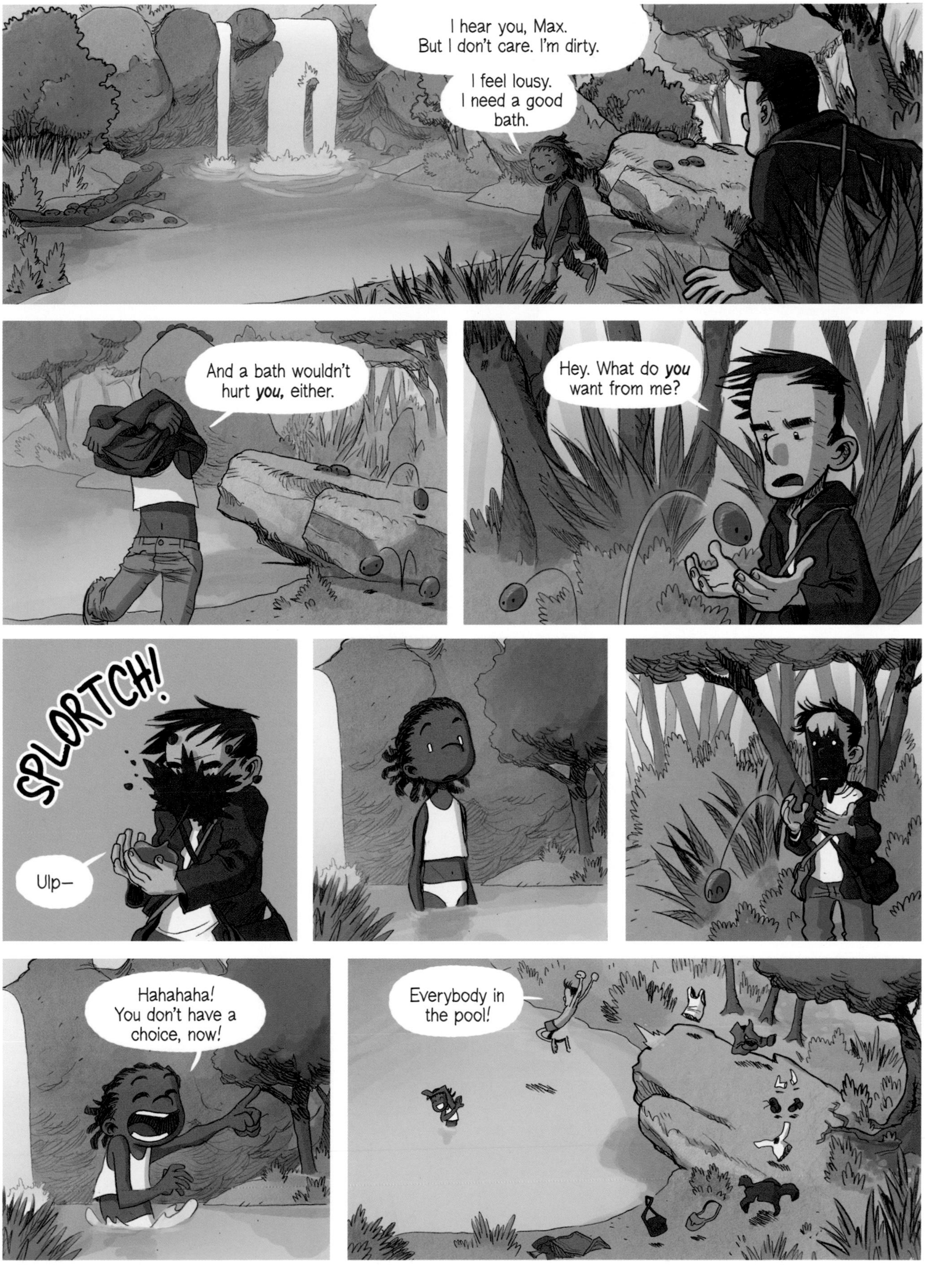

I hear you, Max.
But I don't care. I'm dirty.
I feel lousy.
I need a good bath.
And a bath wouldn't hurt *you,* either.
Hey. What do *you* want from me?
SPLORTCH!
Ulp—
Hahahaha!
You don't have a choice, now!
Everybody in the pool!

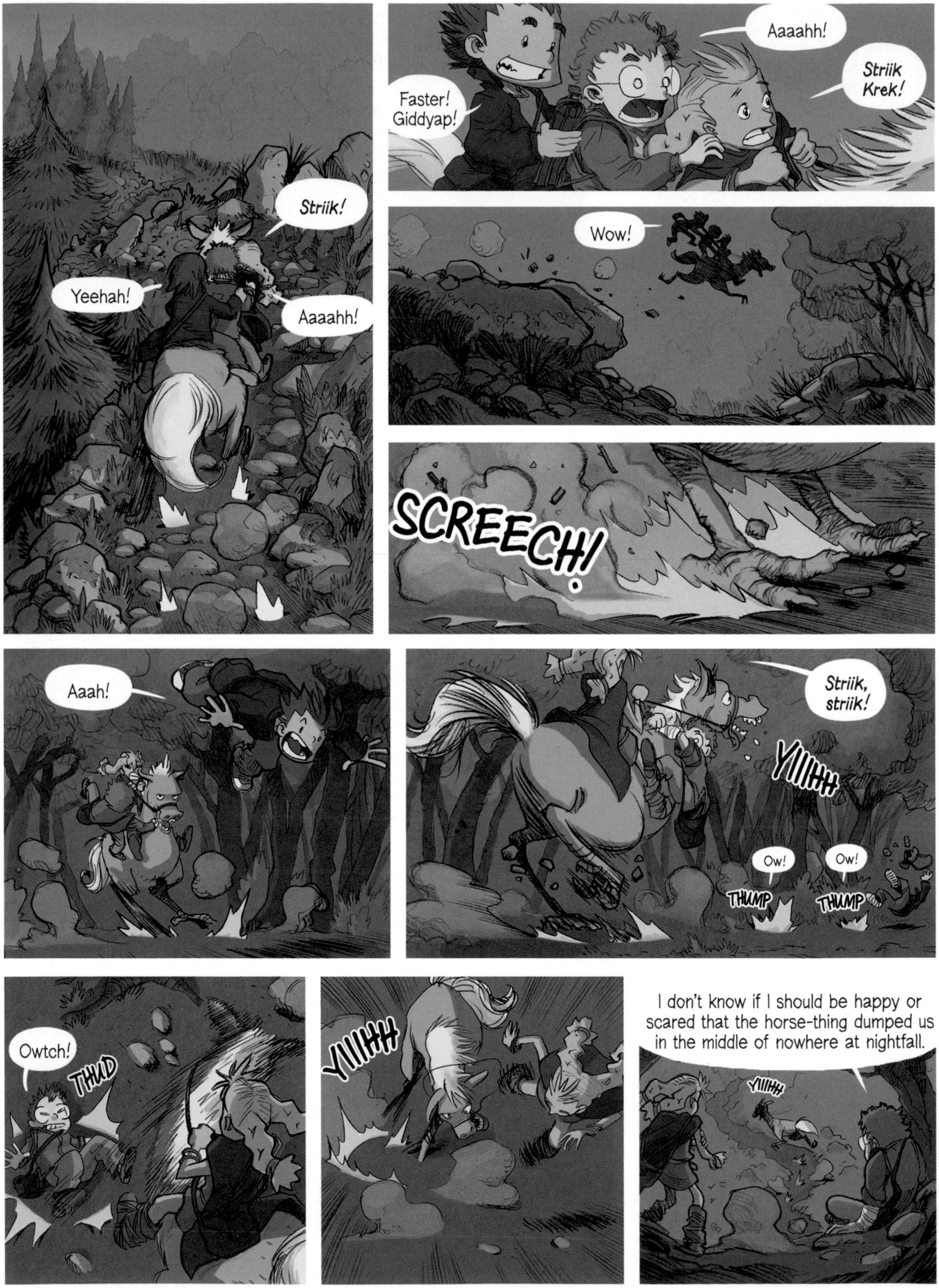
Striik!
Yeehah!
Aaaahh!
Faster! Giddyap!
Aaaahh!
Striik Krek!
Wow!
SCREECH!
Aaah!
Striik, striik!
YIIIHH
Ow!
THUMP
Ow!
THUMP
Owtch!
THUD
YIIIHH
I don't know if I should be happy or scared that the horse-thing dumped us in the middle of nowhere at nightfall.
YIIIHH

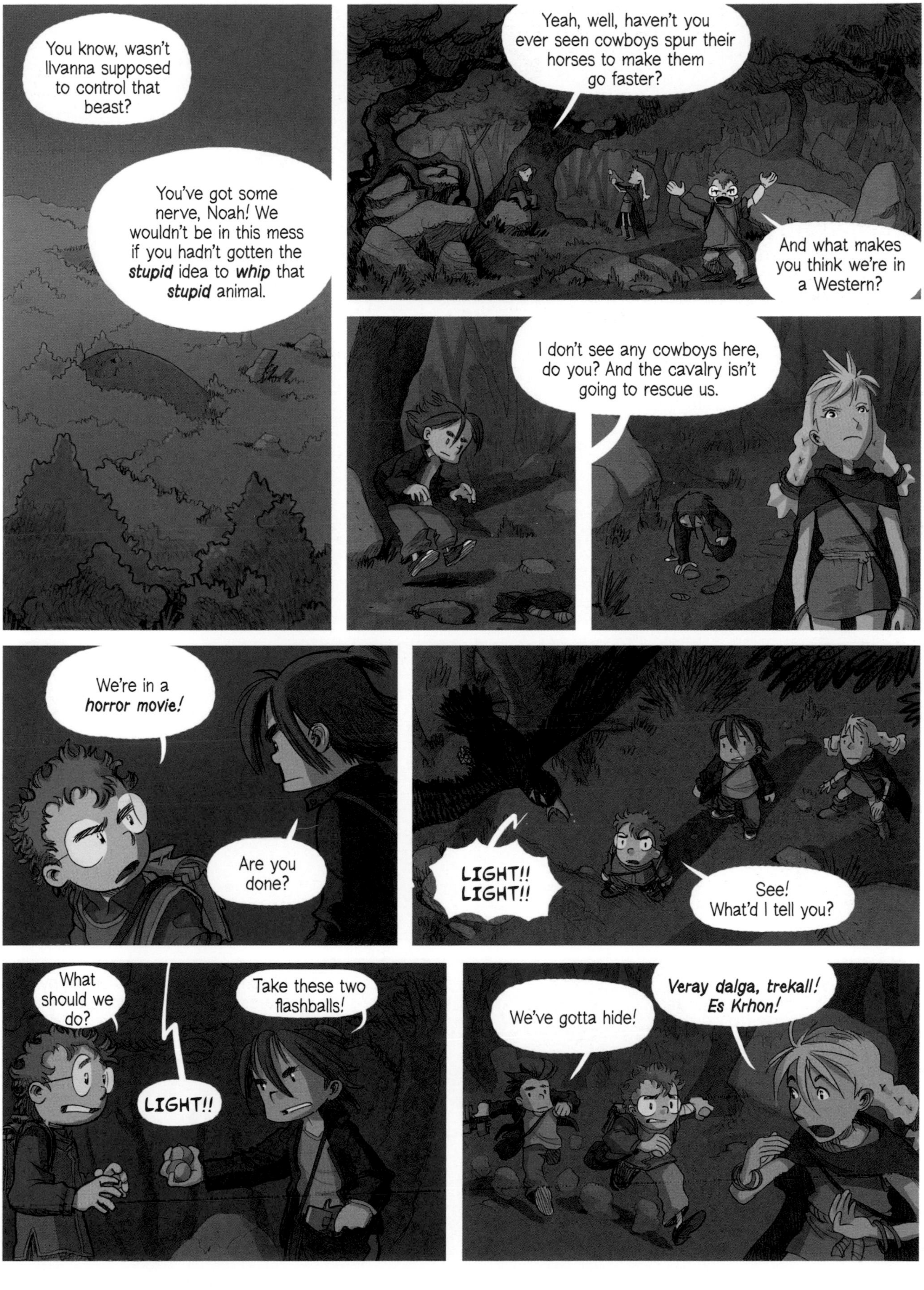
You know, wasn't Ilvanna supposed to control that beast?
You've got some nerve, Noah! We wouldn't be in this mess if you hadn't gotten the ***stupid*** idea to ***whip*** that ***stupid*** animal.
Yeah, well, haven't you ever seen cowboys spur their horses to make them go faster?
And what makes you think we're in a Western?
I don't see any cowboys here, do you? And the cavalry isn't going to rescue us.
We're in a ***horror movie!***
Are you done?
LIGHT!! LIGHT!!
See! What'd I tell you?
What should we do?
LIGHT!!
Take these two flashballs!
We've gotta hide!
Veray dalga, trekall! Es Krhon!

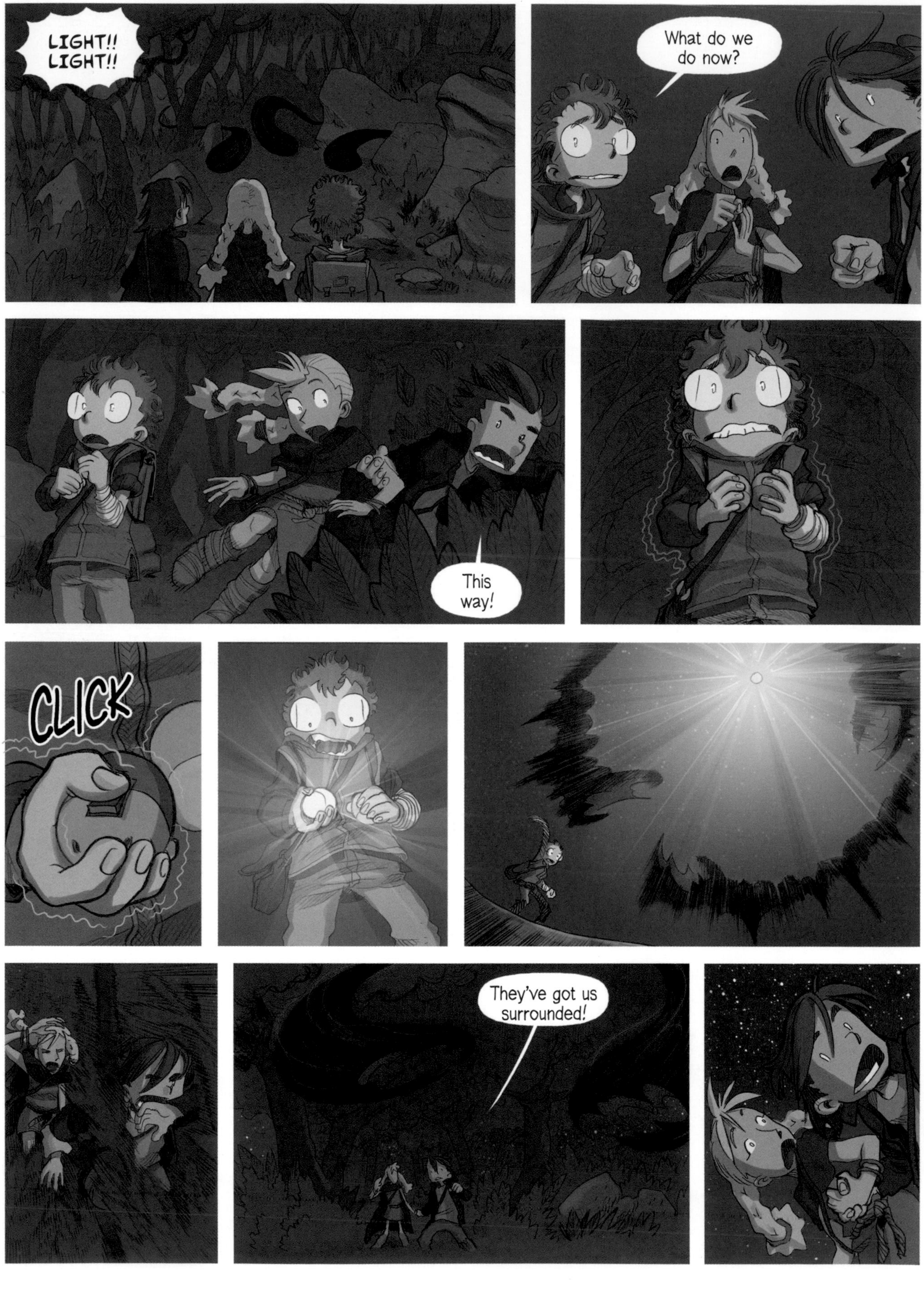
LIGHT!!
LIGHT!!
What do we do now?
This way!
CLICK
They've got us surrounded!

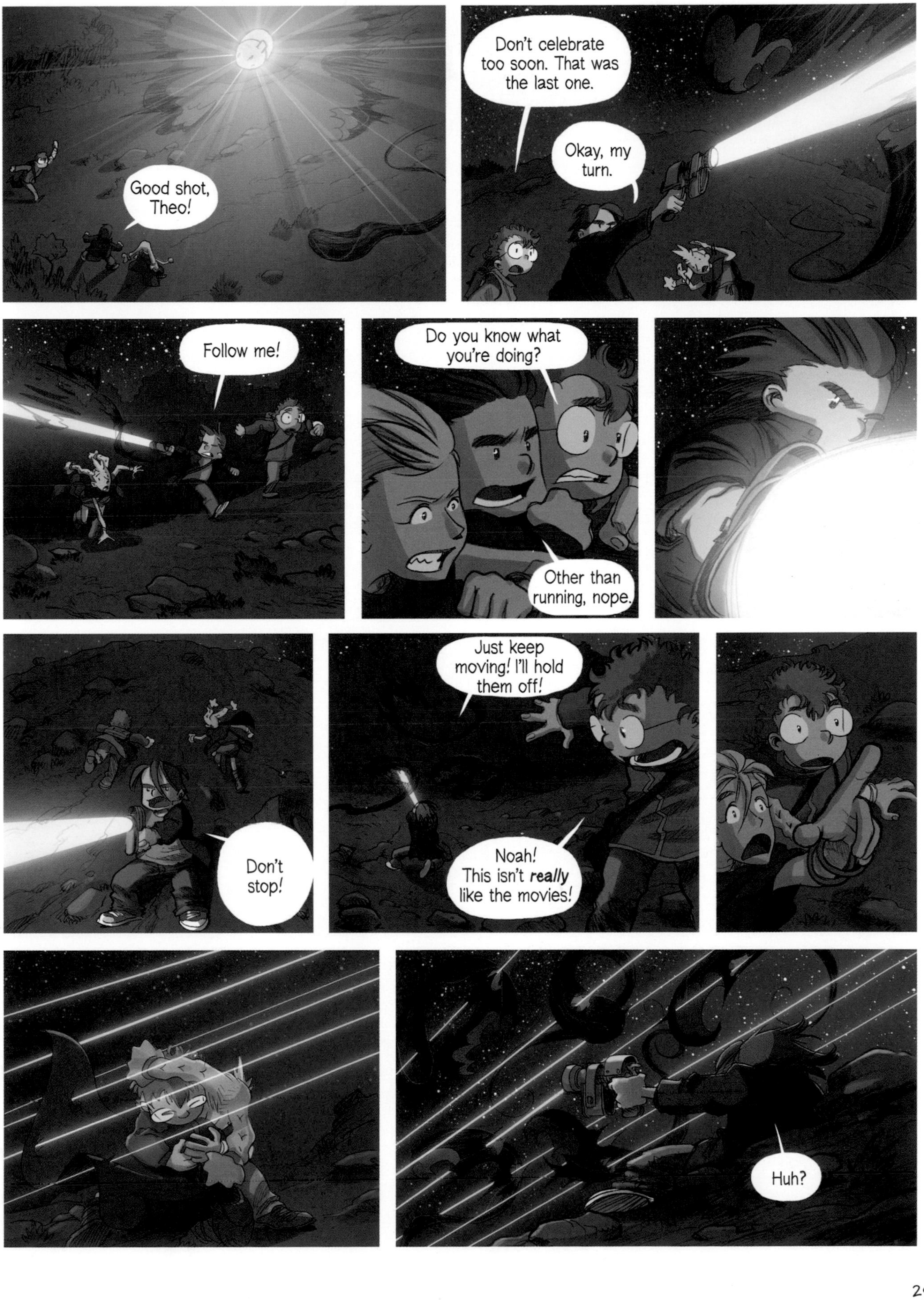
Good shot, Theo!
Don't celebrate too soon. That was the last one.
Okay, my turn.
Follow me!
Do you know what you're doing?
Other than running, nope.
Just keep moving! I'll hold them off!
Don't stop!
Noah! This isn't **really** like the movies!
Huh?

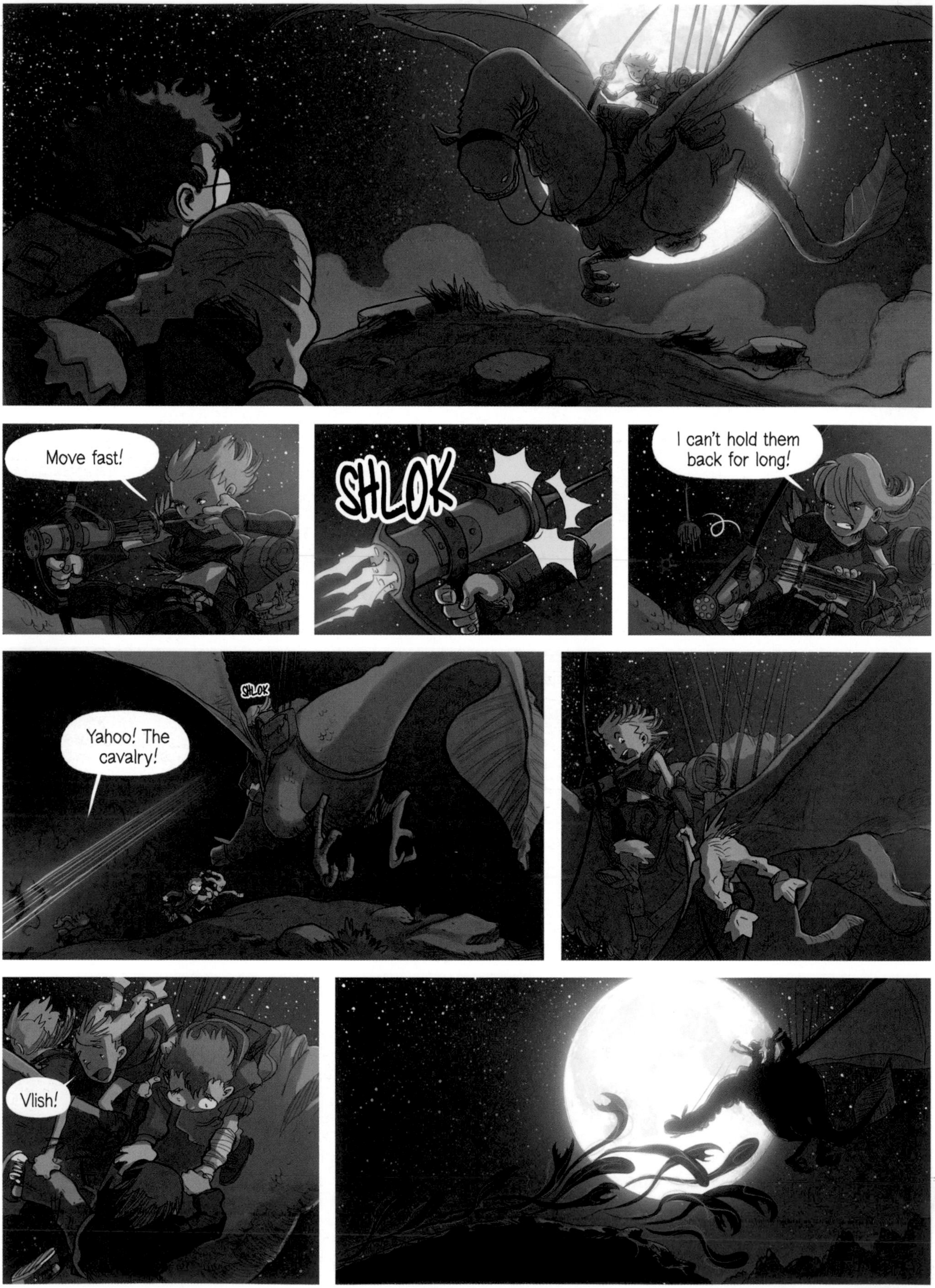
Move fast!
SHLOK
I can't hold them back for long!
SHLOK
Yahoo! The cavalry!
Vlish!

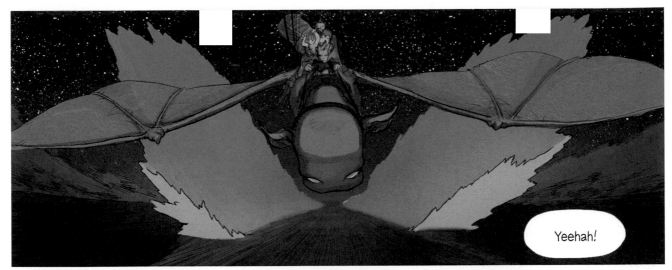

Yeehah!

Noah, you've been yelling in my ear for hours!

Wha-hoo!

The sun's coming up!

I've had enough of this. I'm tired!

Have fun!! This is better than Disneyland—plus it's free! Hahahaha!

Now I know what I want for Christmas.

A dragon!

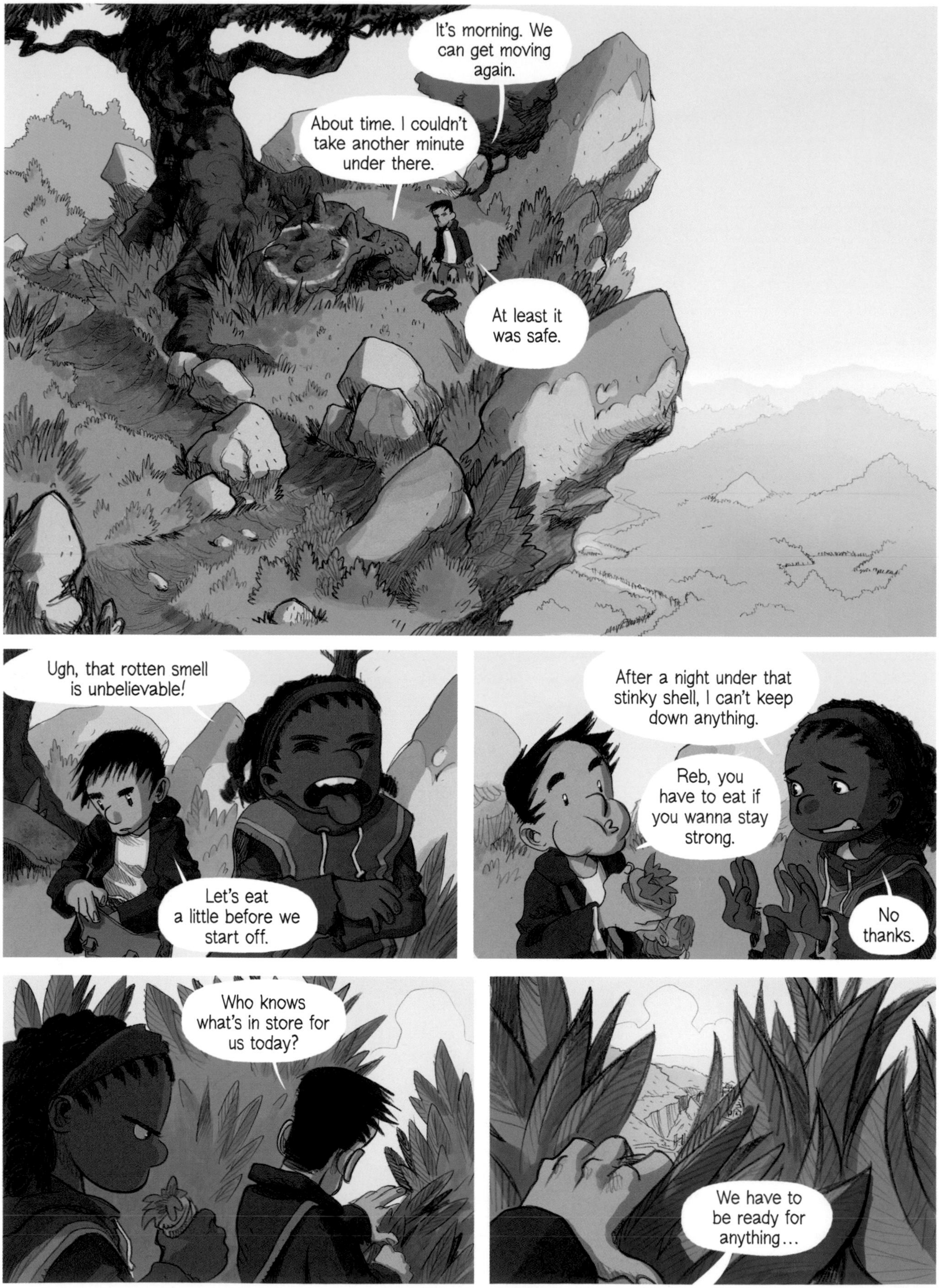
It's morning. We can get moving again.
About time. I couldn't take another minute under there.
At least it was safe.
Ugh, that rotten smell is unbelievable!
Let's eat a little before we start off.
After a night under that stinky shell, I can't keep down anything.
Reb, you have to eat if you wanna stay strong.
No thanks.
Who knows what's in store for us today?
We have to be ready for anything…

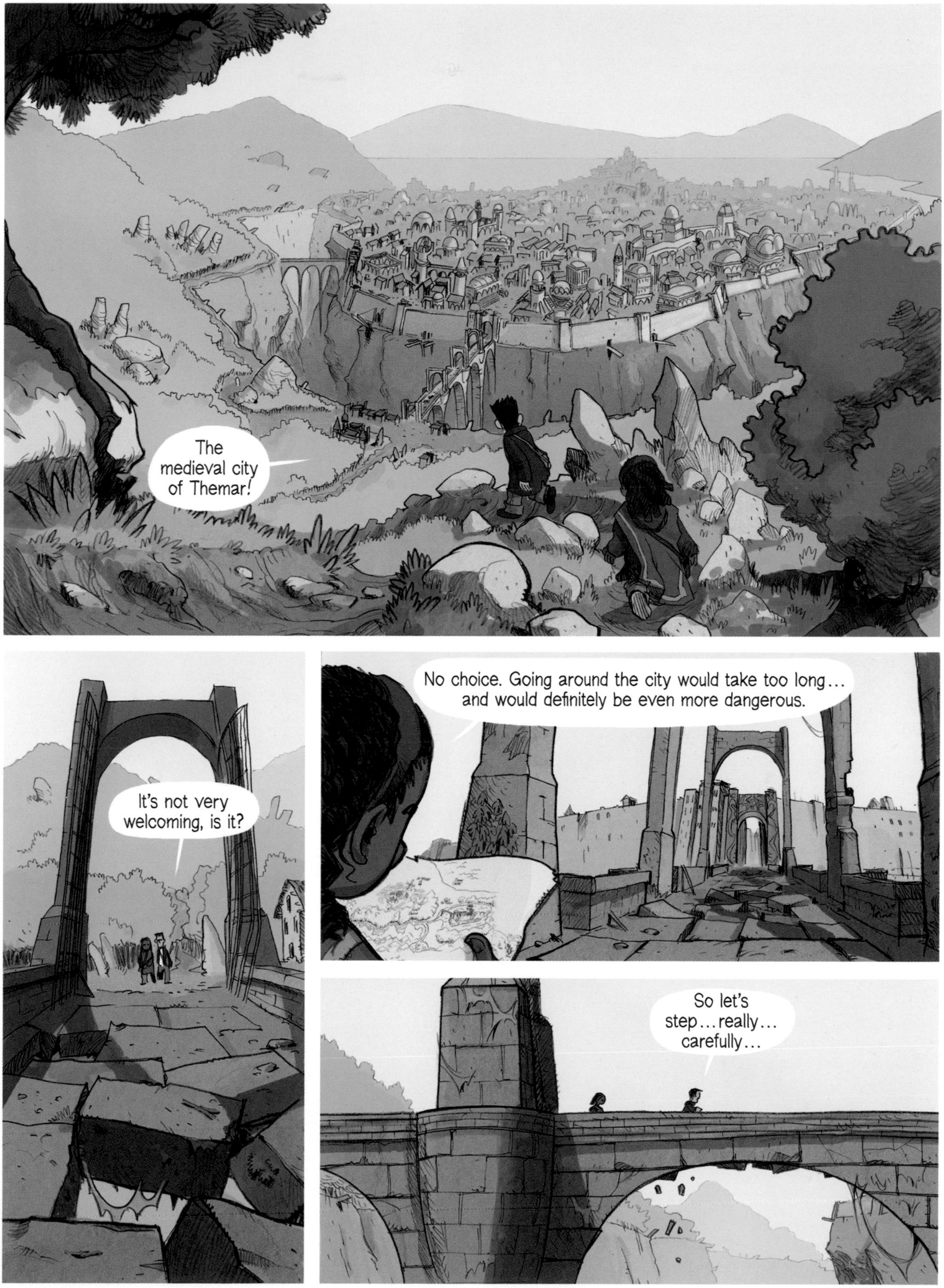
The medieval city of Themar!
It's not very welcoming, is it?
No choice. Going around the city would take too long… and would definitely be even more dangerous.
So let's step… really… carefully…

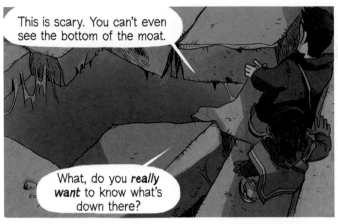

This is scary. You can't even see the bottom of the moat.

What, do you *really want* to know what's down there?

Oh, I think I saw something move!

Just look straight ahead, Reb.

Watch out!

AAH!

I've got you! Don't panic! Stay still, or the hole will get bigger.

Careful... you're almost there...

Oh, Max, I'm scared!

YAAAAARRHH

I'll go first.

What was that sound?

YAAARRHH

Let's not wait around to find out!

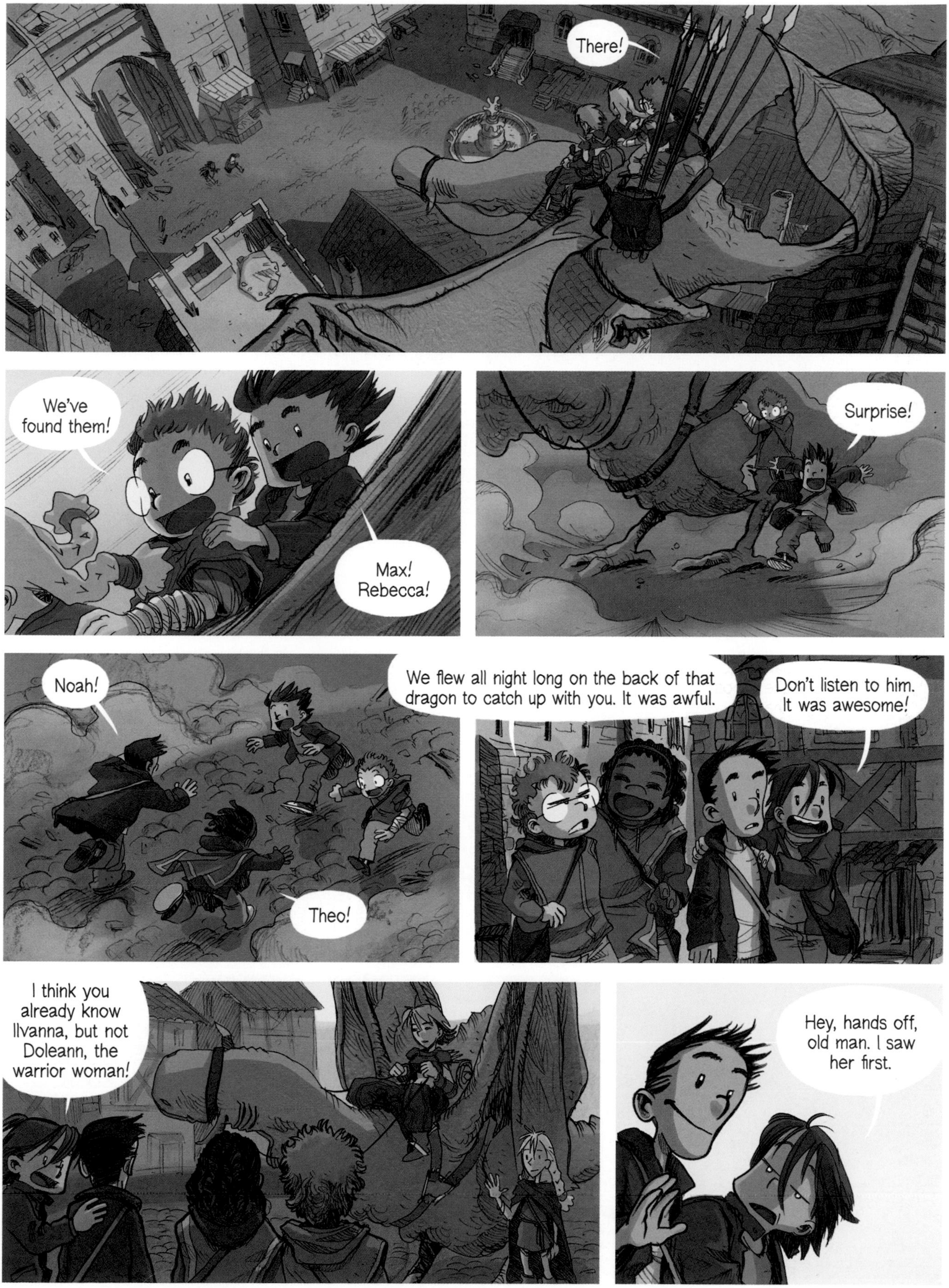
There!
We've found them!
Max! Rebecca!
Surprise!
Noah!
Theo!
We flew all night long on the back of that dragon to catch up with you. It was awful.
Don't listen to him. It was awesome!
I think you already know Ilvanna, but not Doleann, the warrior woman!
Hey, hands off, old man. I saw her first.

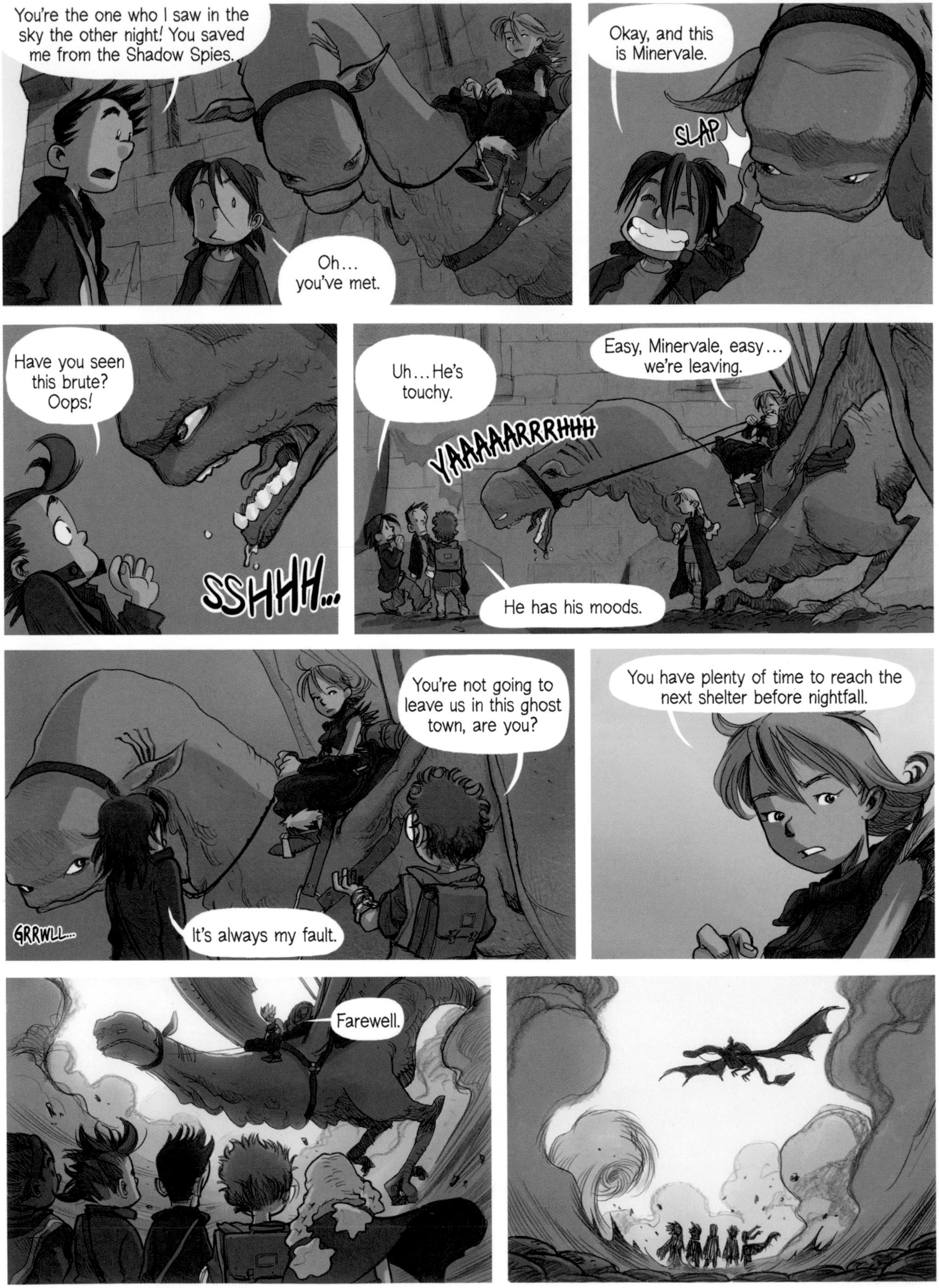

You're the one who I saw in the sky the other night! You saved me from the Shadow Spies.
Oh… you've met.
Okay, and this is Minervale.
SLAP
Have you seen this brute? Oops!
SSHHH…
Uh… He's touchy.
Easy, Minervale, easy… we're leaving.
YAAAAARRRHHH
He has his moods.
You're not going to leave us in this ghost town, are you?
GRRWLL…
It's always my fault.
You have plenty of time to reach the next shelter before nightfall.
Farewell.

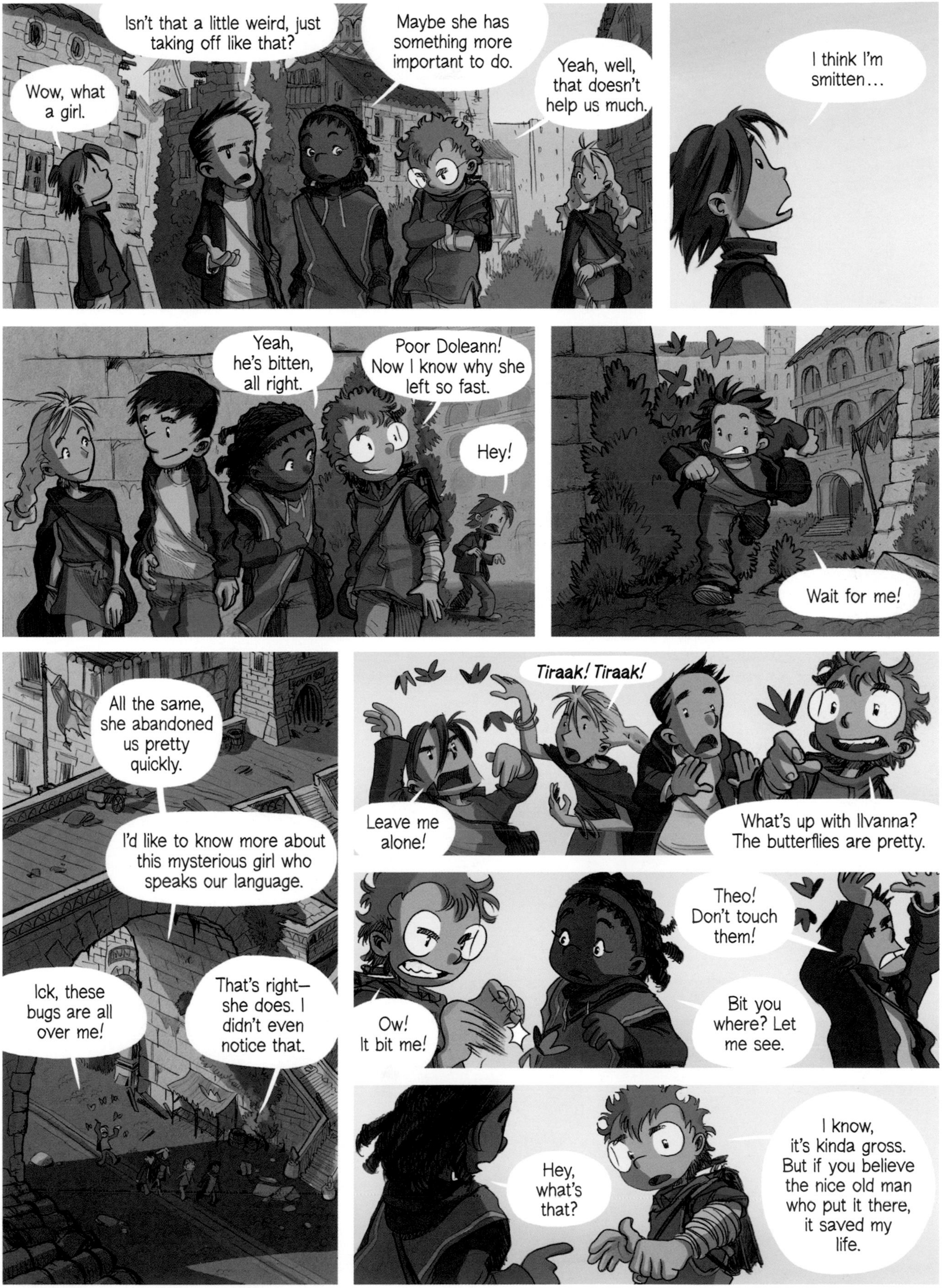
Wow, what a girl.
Isn't that a little weird, just taking off like that?
Maybe she has something more important to do.
Yeah, well, that doesn't help us much.
I think I'm smitten...
Yeah, he's bitten, all right.
Poor Doleann! Now I know why she left so fast.
Hey!
Wait for me!
All the same, she abandoned us pretty quickly.
I'd like to know more about this mysterious girl who speaks our language.
Ick, these bugs are all over me!
That's right— she does. I didn't even notice that.
Tiraak! Tiraak!
Leave me alone!
What's up with Ilvanna? The butterflies are pretty.
Theo! Don't touch them!
Ow! It bit me!
Bit you where? Let me see.
Hey, what's that?
I know, it's kinda gross. But if you believe the nice old man who put it there, it saved my life.

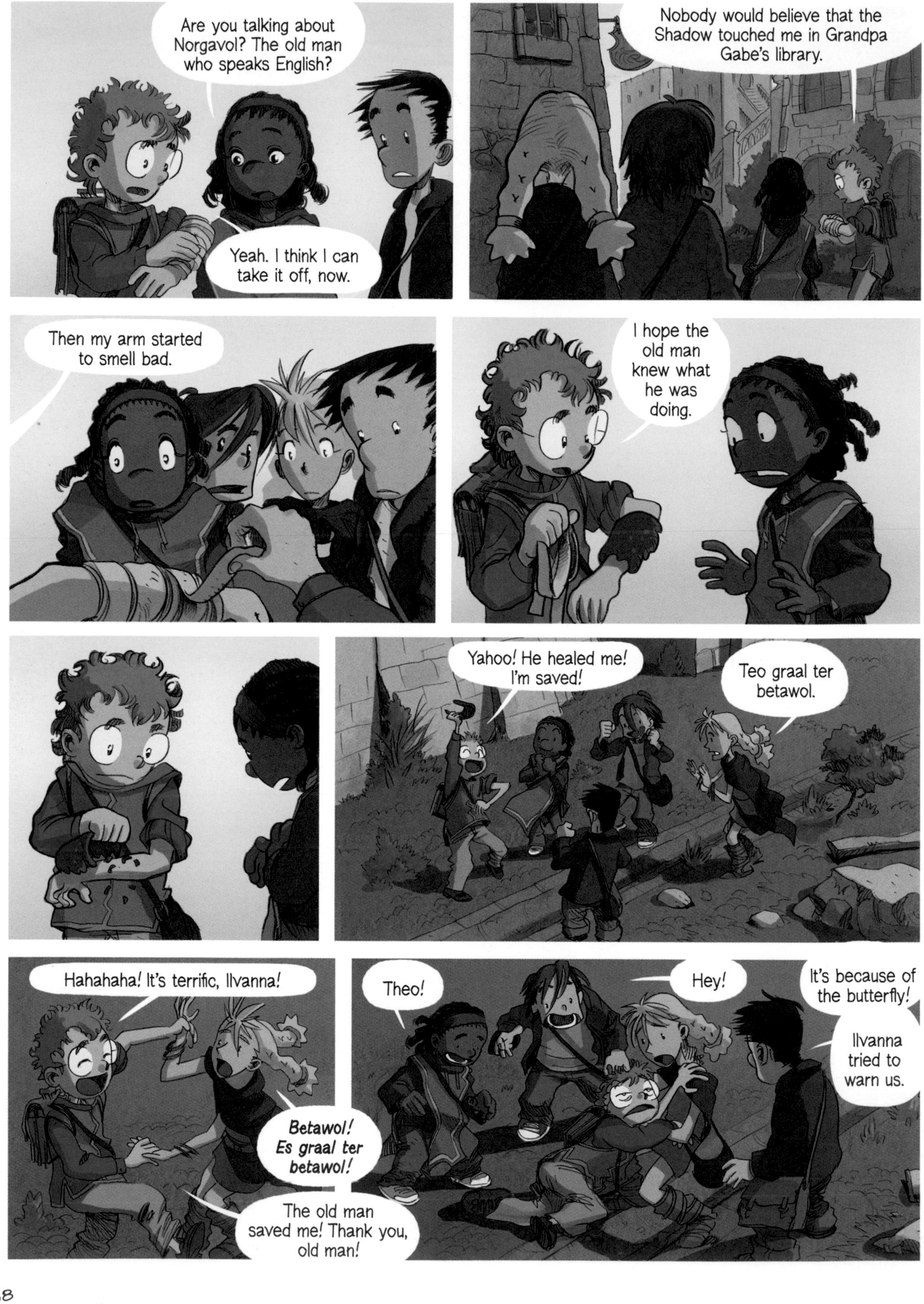

Are you talking about Norgavol? The old man who speaks English?
Yeah. I think I can take it off, now.
Nobody would believe that the Shadow touched me in Grandpa Gabe's library.
Then my arm started to smell bad.
I hope the old man knew what he was doing.
Yahoo! He healed me! I'm saved!
Teo graal ter betawol.
Hahahaha! It's terrific, Ilvanna!
Betawol! Es graal ter betawol!
The old man saved me! Thank you, old man!
Theo!
Hey!
It's because of the butterfly!
Ilvanna tried to warn us.

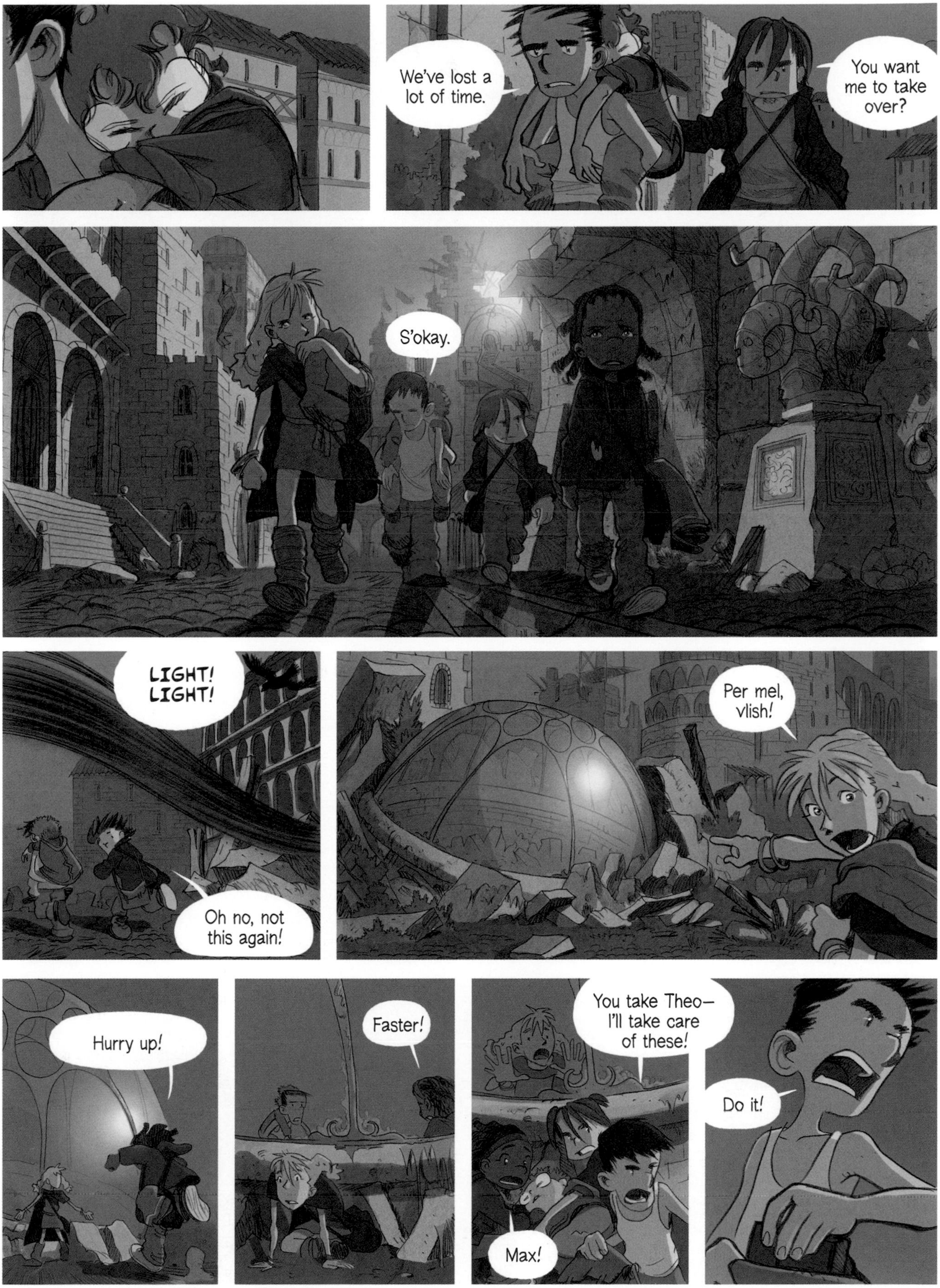
We've lost a lot of time.
You want me to take over?
S'okay.
LIGHT! LIGHT!
Oh no, not this again!
Per mel, vlish!
Hurry up!
Faster!
You take Theo— I'll take care of these!
Max!
Do it!

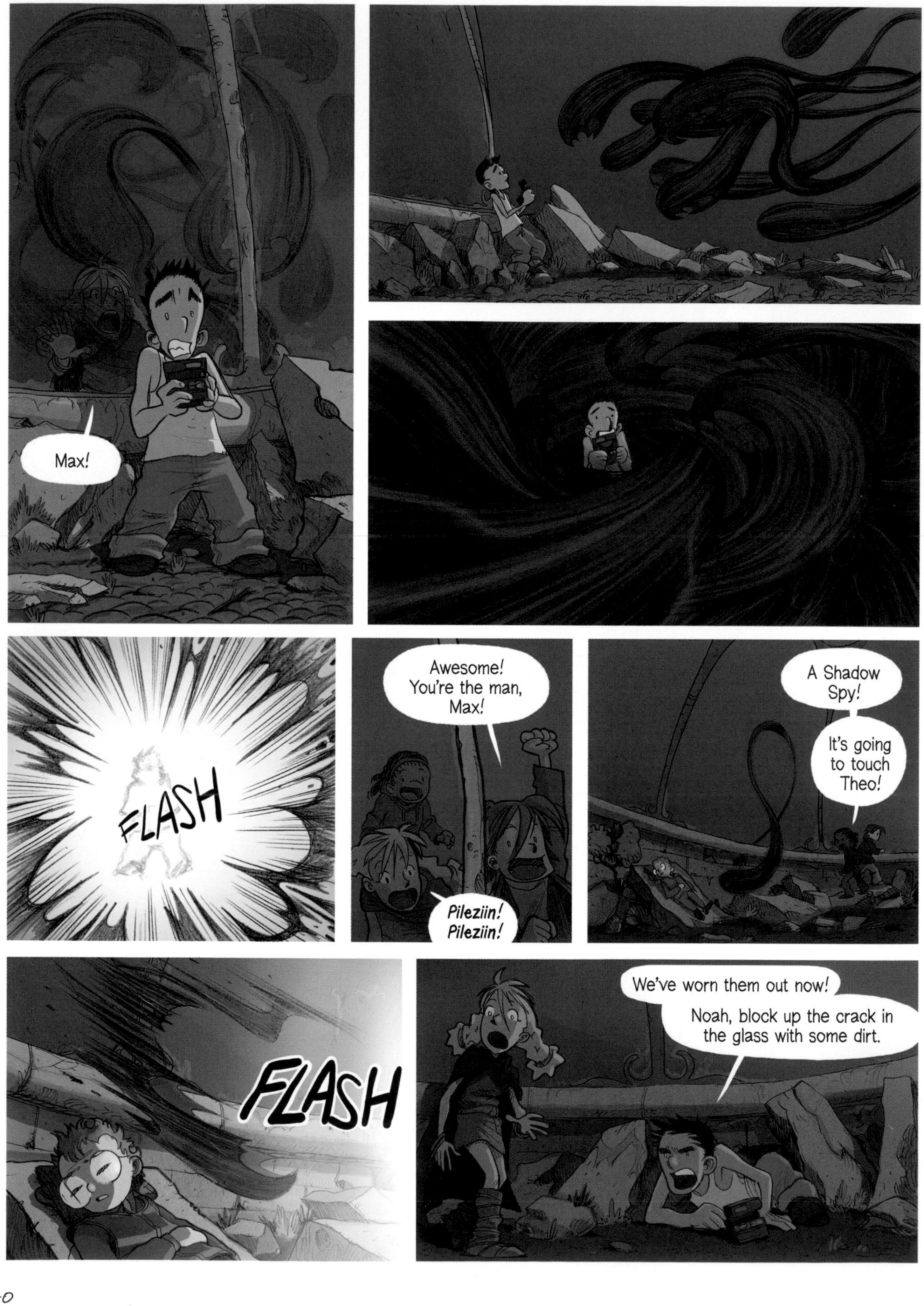
Max!
FLASH
Awesome! You're the man, Max!
Pileziin! Pileziin!
A Shadow Spy!
It's going to touch Theo!
FLASH
We've worn them out now!
Noah, block up the crack in the glass with some dirt.

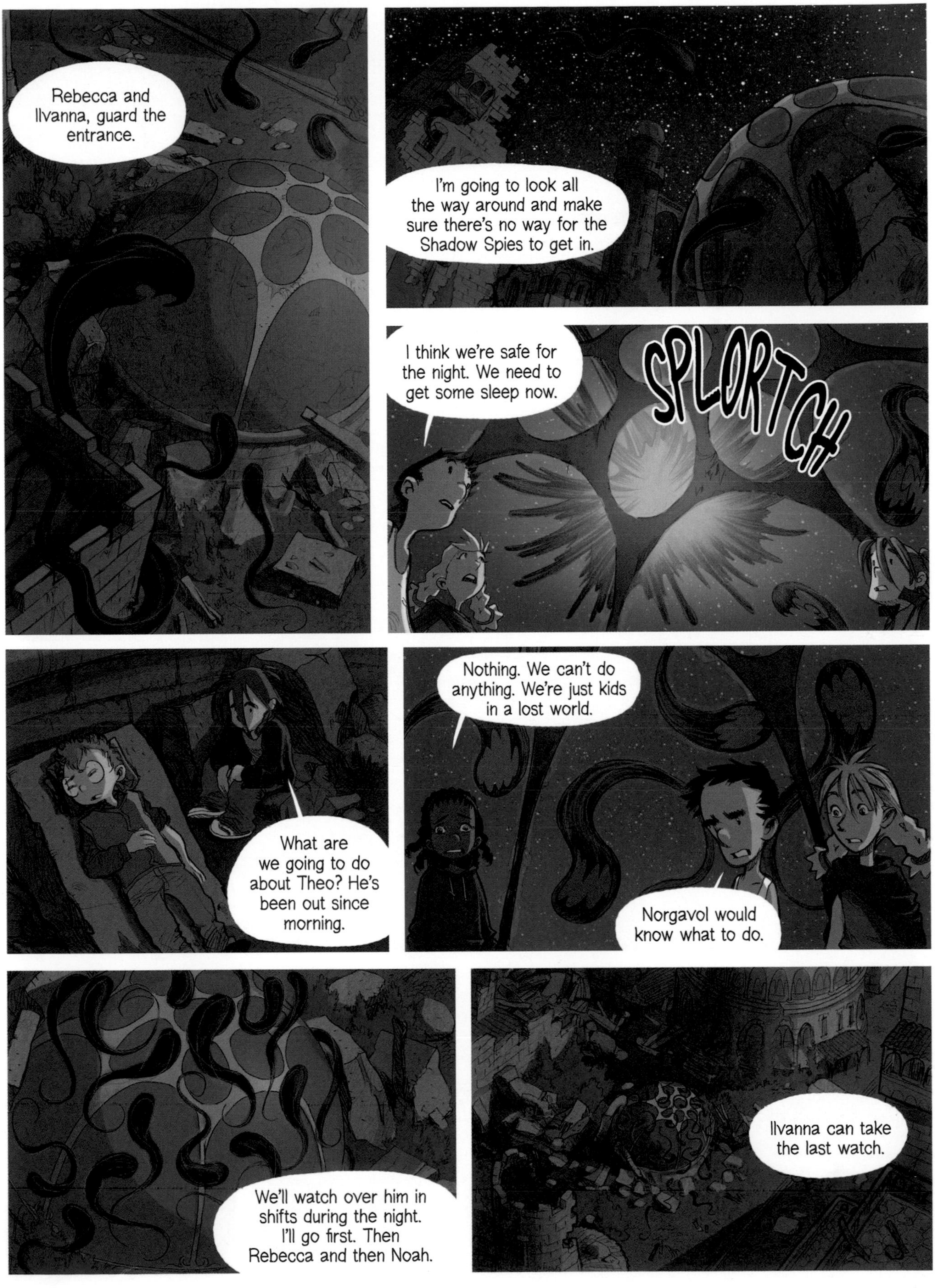
Rebecca and Ilvanna, guard the entrance.
I'm going to look all the way around and make sure there's no way for the Shadow Spies to get in.
I think we're safe for the night. We need to get some sleep now.
SPLORTCH
What are we going to do about Theo? He's been out since morning.
Nothing. We can't do anything. We're just kids in a lost world.
Norgavol would know what to do.
We'll watch over him in shifts during the night. I'll go first. Then Rebecca and then Noah.
Ilvanna can take the last watch.

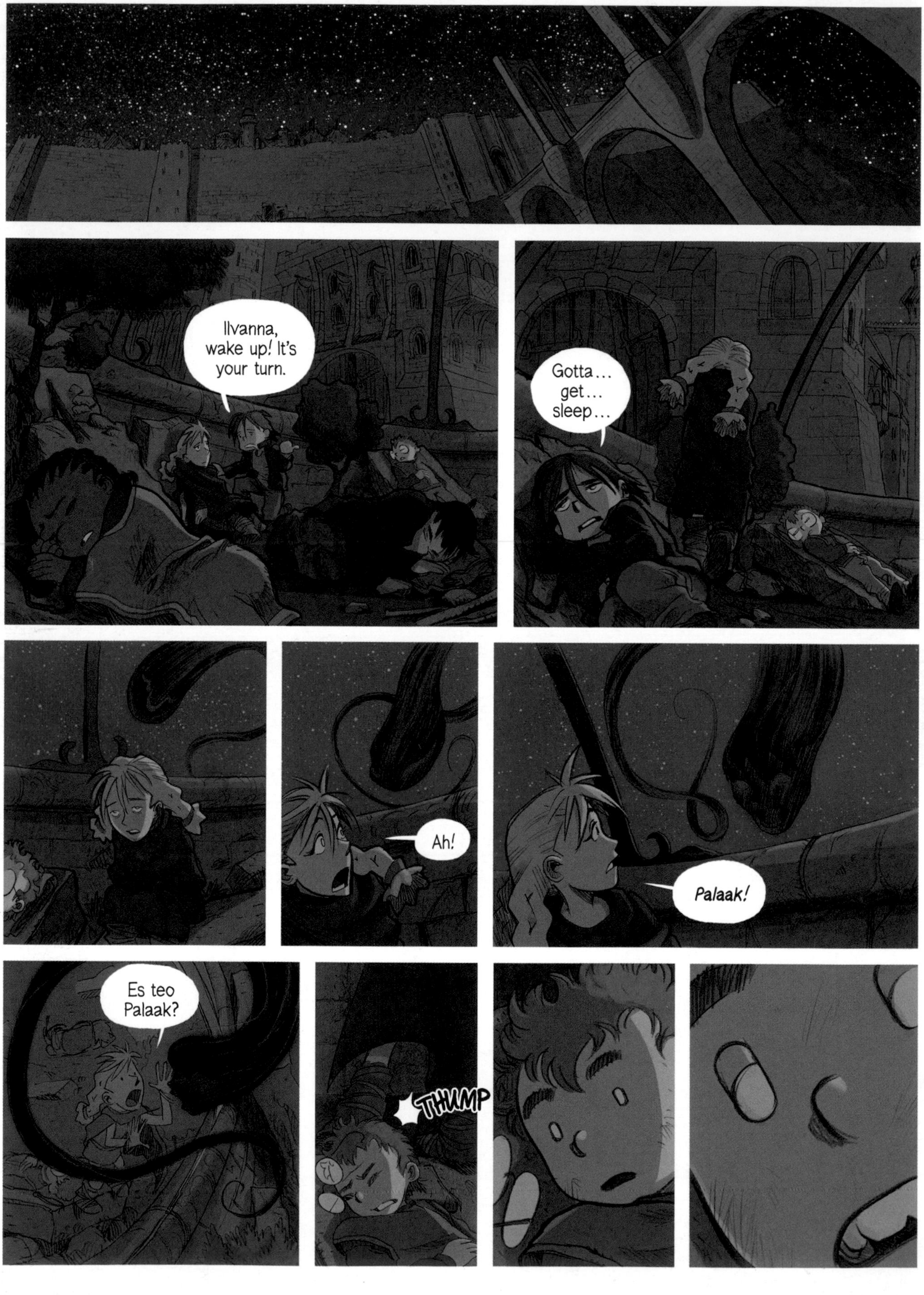
Ilvanna, wake up! It's your turn.
Gotta... get... sleep...
Ah!
Palaak!
Es teo Palaak?
THUMP

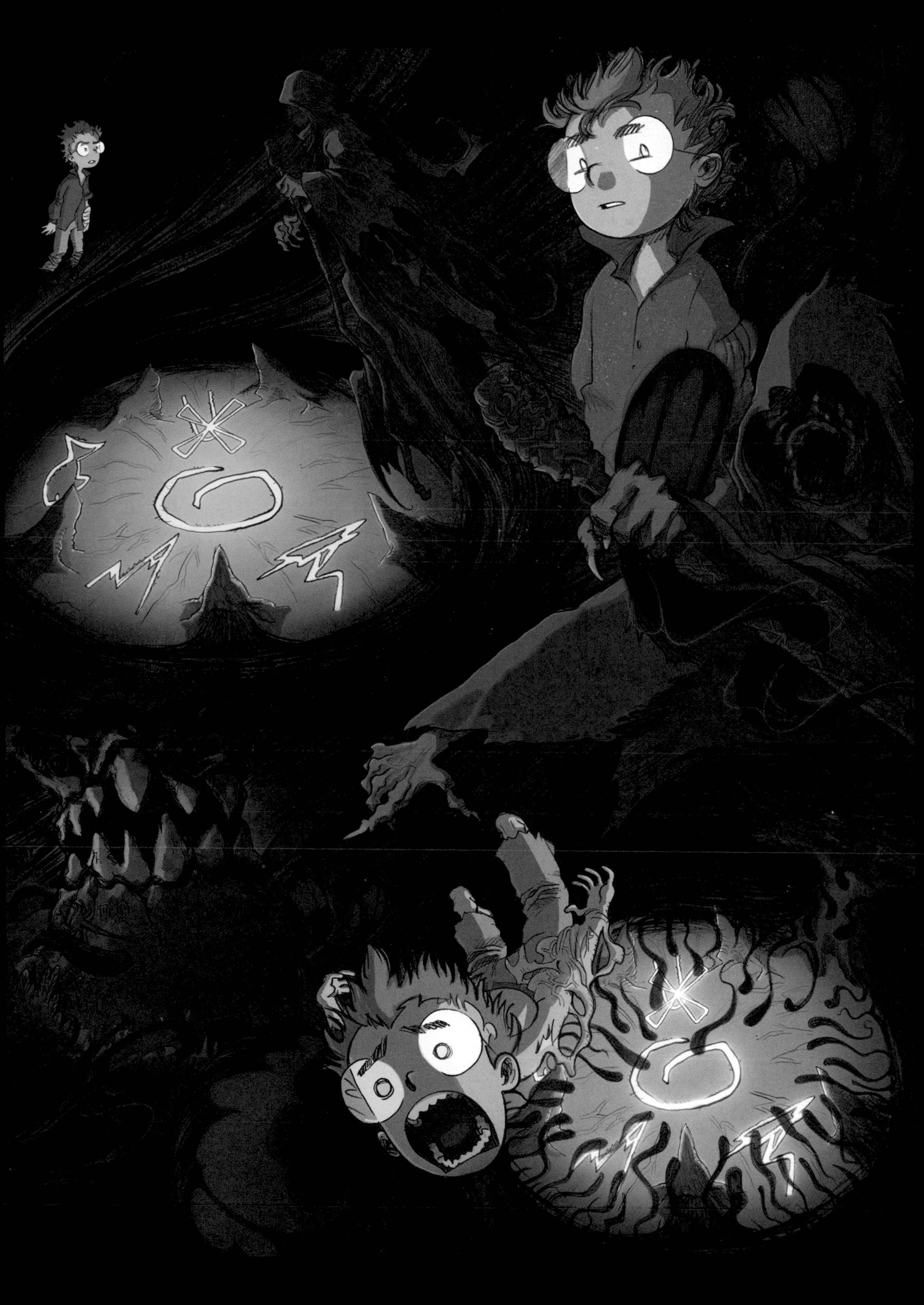

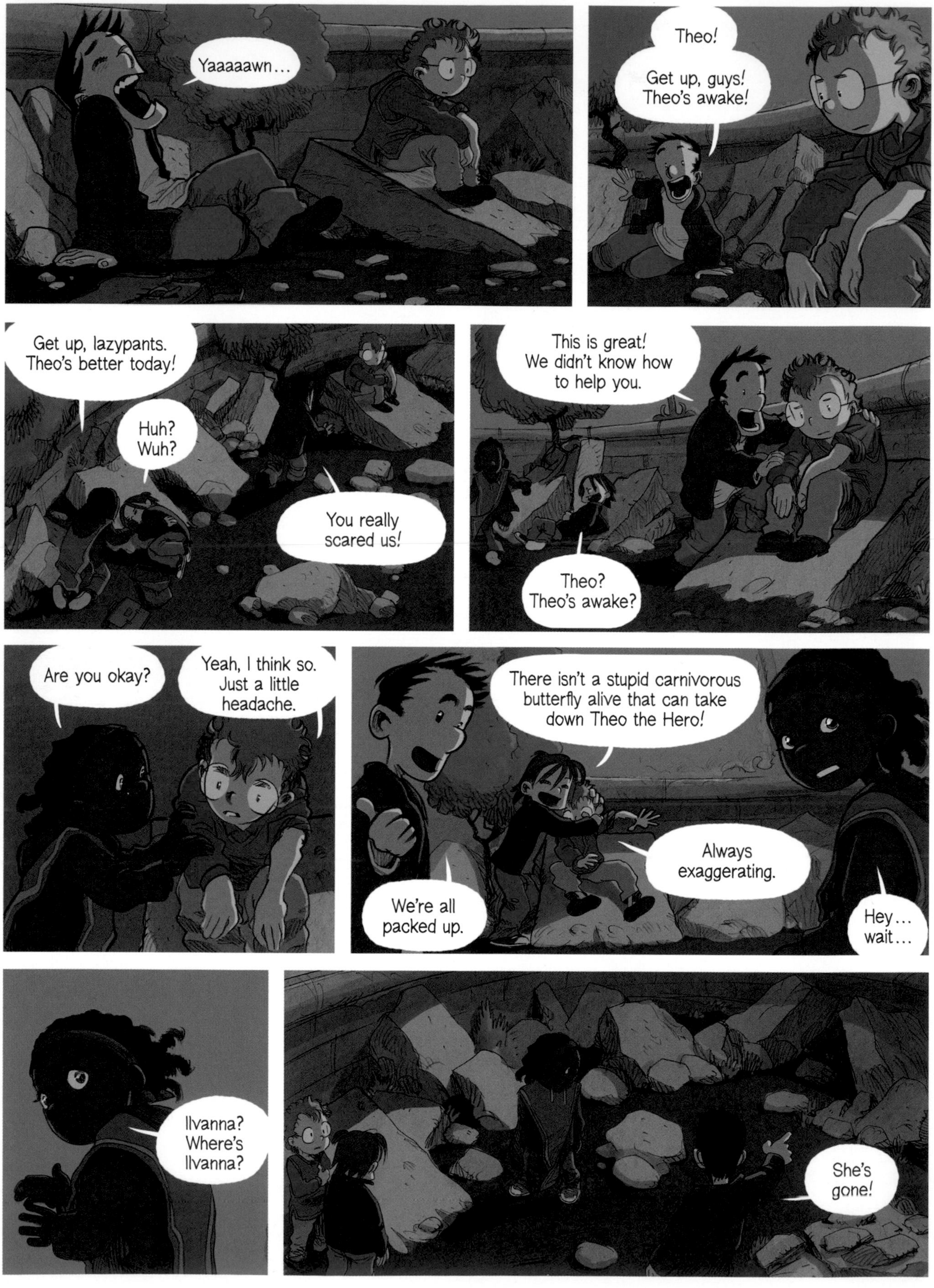
Yaaaaawn...
Theo!
Get up, guys! Theo's awake!
Get up, lazypants. Theo's better today!
Huh? Wuh?
You really scared us!
This is great! We didn't know how to help you.
Theo? Theo's awake?
Are you okay?
Yeah, I think so. Just a little headache.
There isn't a stupid carnivorous butterfly alive that can take down Theo the Hero!
We're all packed up.
Always exaggerating.
Hey... wait...
Ilvanna? Where's Ilvanna?
She's gone!

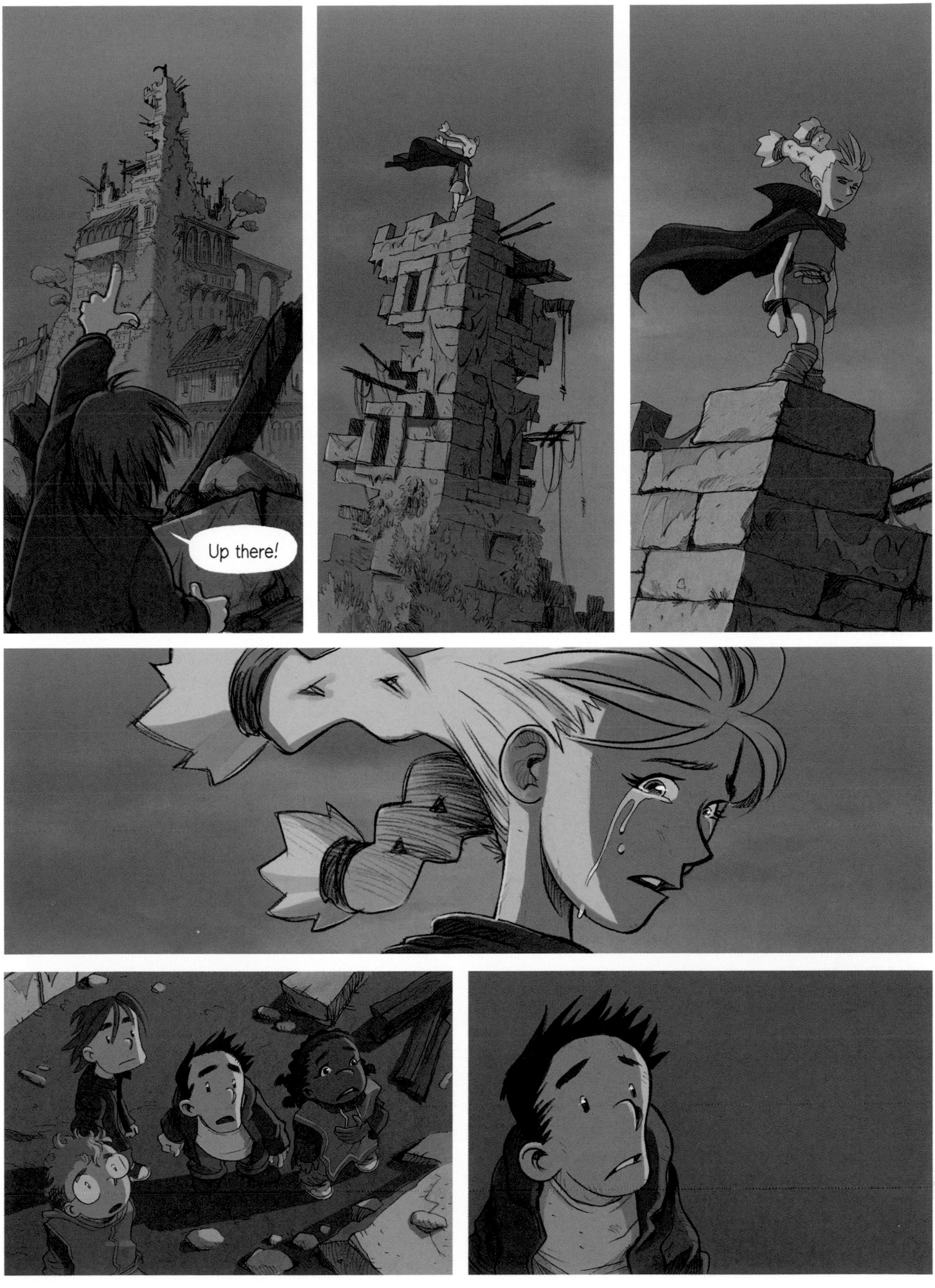
Up there!

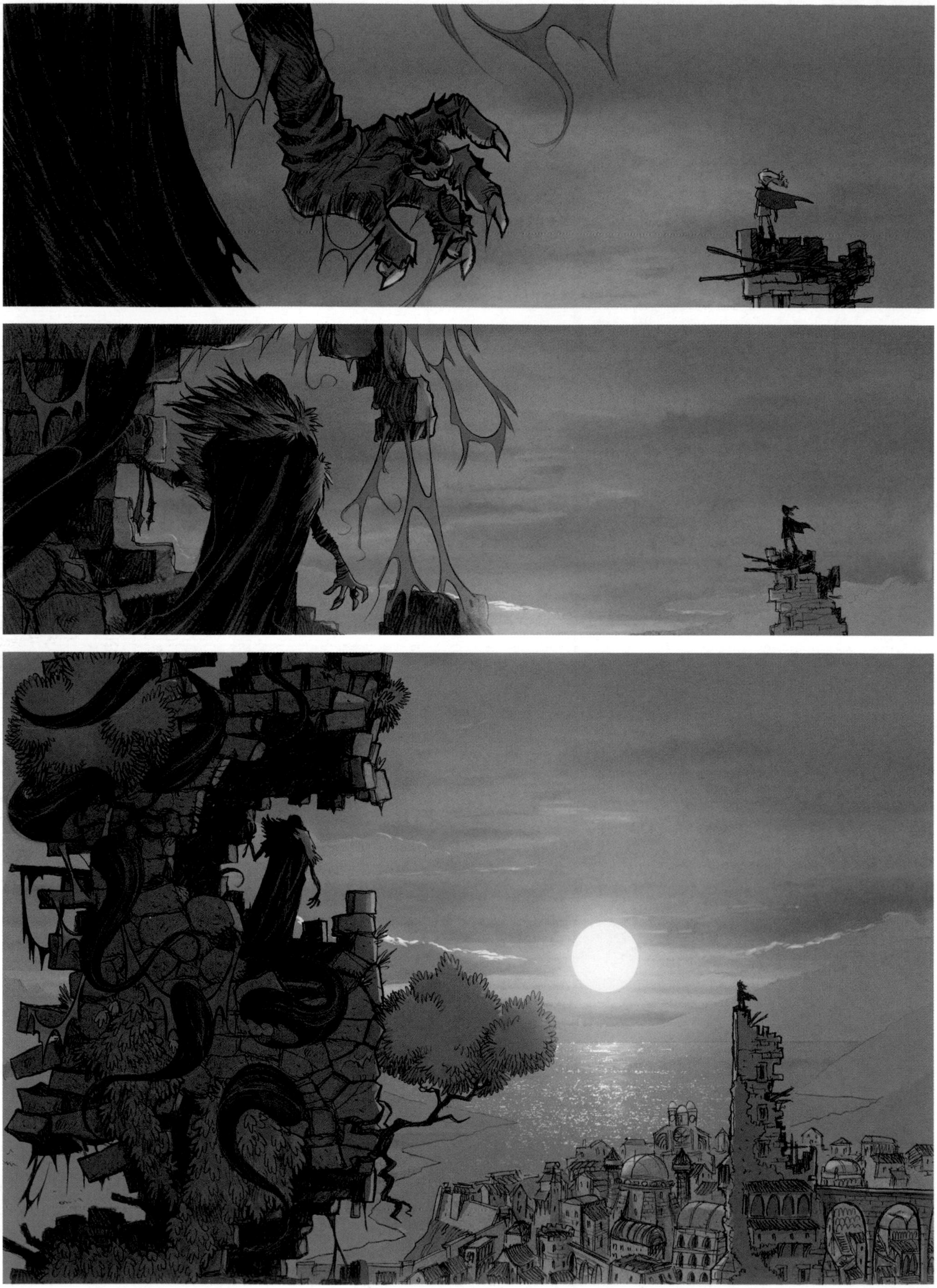

NEXT EPISODE...

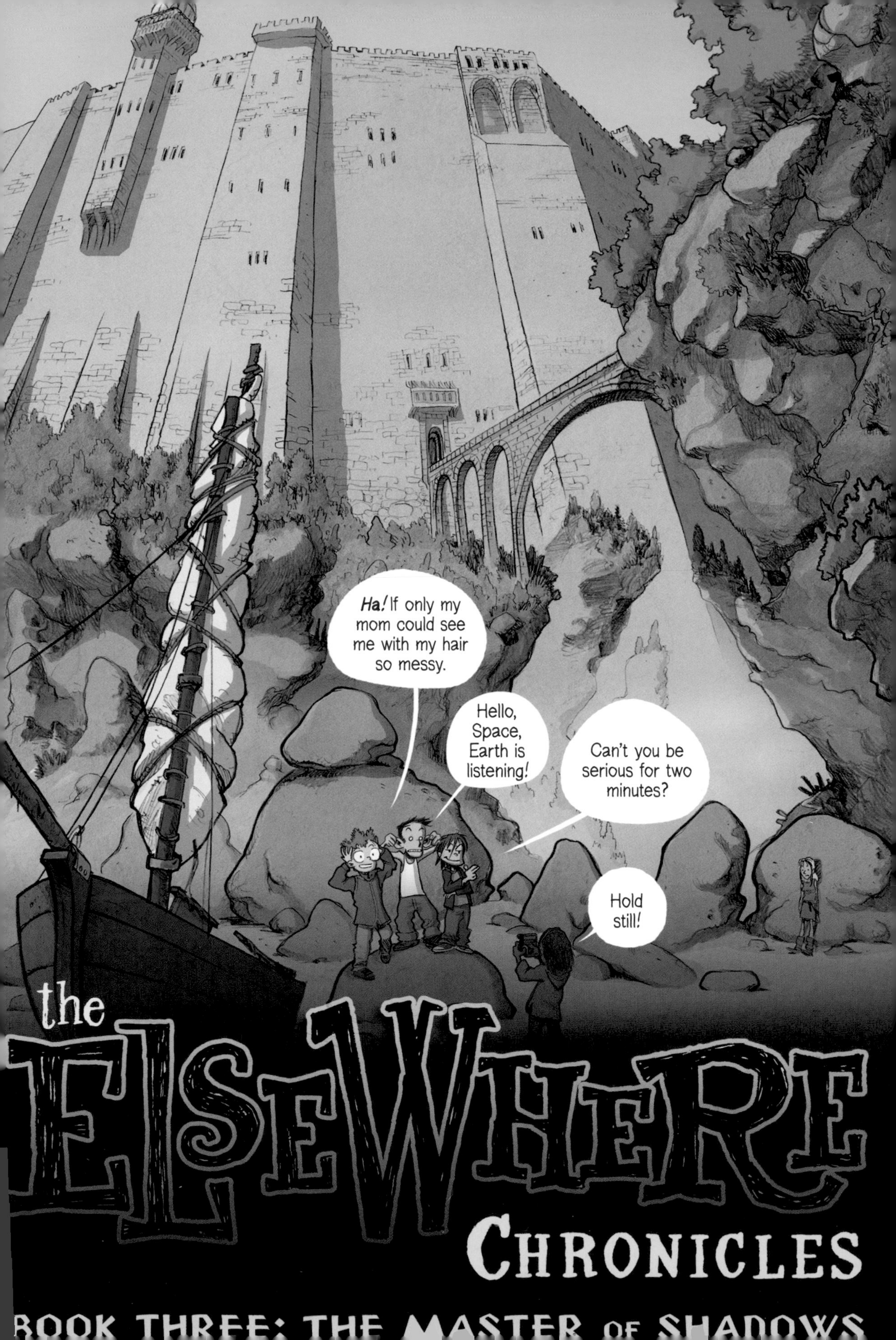
Ha! If only my mom could see me with my hair so messy.
Hello, Space, Earth is listening!
Can't you be serious for two minutes?
Hold still!
the ElseWhere Chronicles
BOOK THREE: THE MASTER OF SHADOWS

Art by Bannister
Story by Nykko
Colors by Jaffré
Translation by Carol Klio Burrell

First American edition published in 2009 by Graphic Universe™.
Published by arrangement with S.A. DUPUIS, Belgium.

Graphic Universe™
A division of Lerner Publishing Group, Inc.
241 First Avenue North
Minneapolis, MN 55401 USA

For reading levels and more information, look up this title at www.lernerbooks.com.

Library of Congress Cataloging-in-Publication Data

Bannister.
[Ombres. English]
The Shadow Spies / art by Bannister ; story by Nykko ; [colors by Jaffré ;
translation by Carol Klio Burrell]. — 1st American ed.
    p.   cm. — (The ElseWhere chronicles ; bk. 2)
Summary: Rebecca, Max, Theo, and Noah continue their journey through the other world
in search of a way home, pursued by the Shadow Spies and the mysterious Master of Shadows.
ISBN: 978-0-7613-4460-5 (lib. bdg. : alk. paper)
1. Graphic novels. [1. Graphic novels. 2. Horror stories.] I. Nykko. II. Jaffré.
III. Burrell, Carol Klio. IV. Title.
PZ7.7.B34Sm 2009
741.5'973—dc22   2008039443

Manufactured in the United States of America
6 - 36564 - 10414 - 10/26/2018

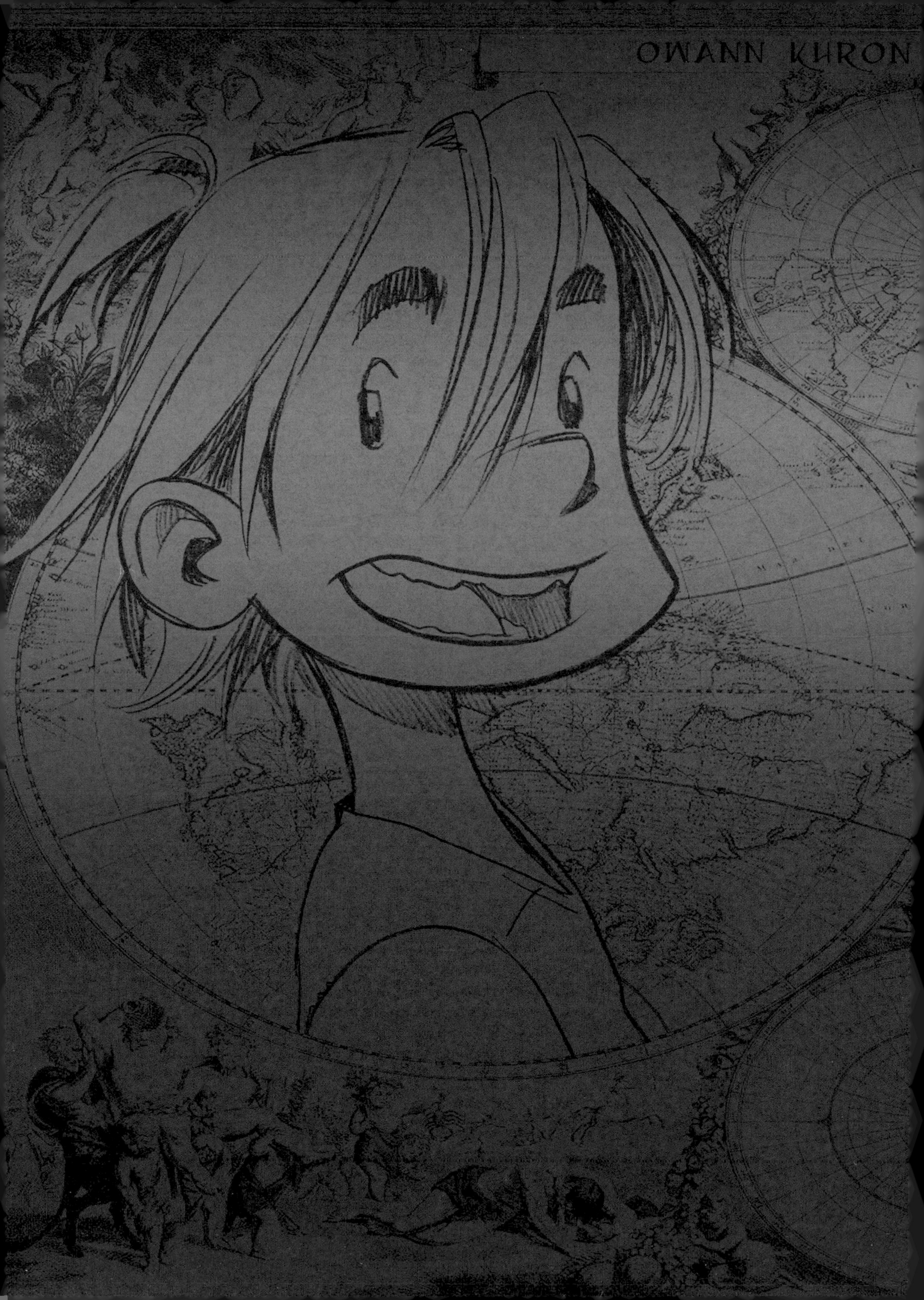
OWANN KURON

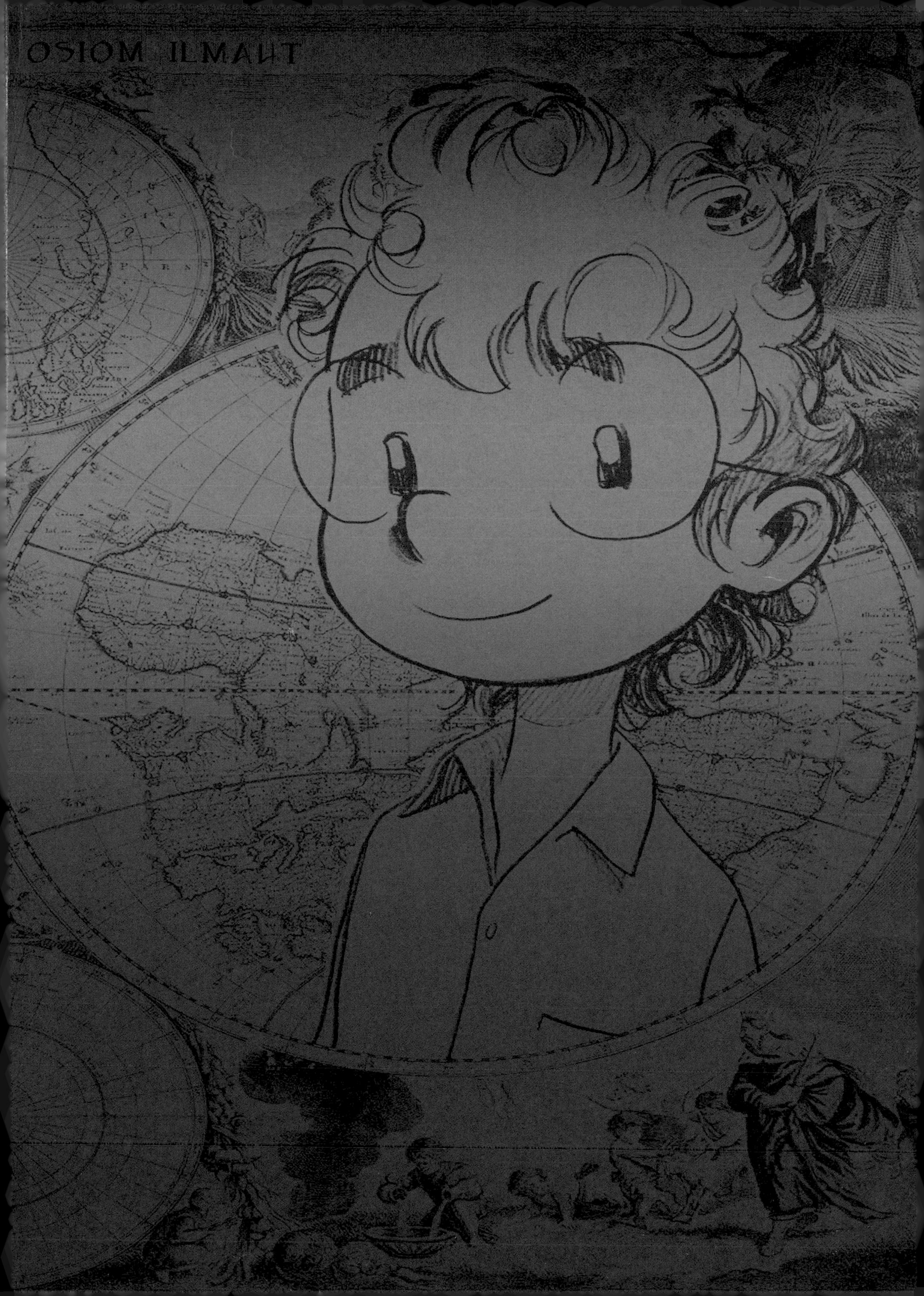